POLICE PROCEDURALS RESPECTED BY LAW ENFORCEMENT.™

"Carolyn Arnold provides entertainment and accuracy."
—*Michael D. Scott, Patrolman (Ret.), Castroville, Texas*

"Carolyn Arnold writes realistic and entertaining police procedurals with characters so real, I lose myself in her books."
—*Deputy Rebecca Hendrix, LeFlore County Sheriff's Department, Poteau, Oklahoma*

"For Police procedurals that are painstakingly researched and accurately portrayed look no further than Carolyn Arnold's works. The only way it gets more real than this is to leave the genre completely."
—*Zach Fortier, Police Officer (Ret.), Colorado, United States*

ALSO BY CAROLYN ARNOLD

THE DEFENSELESS

CAROLYN ARNOLD

HIBBERT
&
STILES
PUBLISHING INC.

The Defenseless (Book 3 in the Brandon Fisher FBI series)
Copyright © 2014 by Carolyn Arnold

Excerpt from *Blue Baby* (Book 4 in the Brandon Fisher FBI series) copyright ©
2015 by Carolyn Arnold

www.carolynarnold.net

2015 Hibbert & Stiles Publishing Inc. Edition

ISBN (e-book): 978-0-9878400-7-3
ISBN (print): 978-1-988064-08-6

Cover design: WGA Designs

Prologue

Twenty-six years ago

HE SHOULD BE CELEBRATING AT home with a bottle of Cristal. Instead, he was outside of his neighbor's house, frozen to the bone, his hands like ice.

He hadn't had a moment of peace and quiet all day. His project was getting further behind, the deadline ever looming, but the new resident next door gave no consideration to those around him. First it was his barking dog, but when he came to complain, the sight of it whelmed up pity into his heart and fueled his rage toward its owner.

With the canine now tucked away back at his home, warm and secure, he trudged back out through the snow.

The heavy-metal music that had drowned out the howls of the animal, now vibrated the deck.

All he needed was silence. So he could think. So he could get what he needed to get done, done.

He pounded on the door, and it sent pain flashing through his knuckles—the combination of determination and the bitter temperatures against flesh and bone.

The wind howled between the two houses, gusting up the snow into miniature funnel clouds of ice crystals. They assaulted any bared skin—his neck and face taking the brunt of it. A quiver wracked his body and prompted a deep exhalation, which created a cloud of white in the night air.

"Open the fucking door!" He pushed through the discomfort and knocked again.

Still no evidence the man was even listening.

He surveyed, left and right, glancing over his shoulder, feeling eyes on him. Were the neighbors watching him? Did they call the cops?

The light was on in an upstairs room, but otherwise the nearby house was enshrouded in darkness. The only other illumination were the streetlights that cast dull beacons amidst the blowing snow.

He went to bang again, but his hands refused. They had seized up from the cold. He blew on them to warm them. Surely, the occupant was drunk and would awaken from his stupor to—

The door opened and with it, the music got louder.

"What the fuck do you want?" The man stood there, six feet tall, a few inches shy of his own height, and his face was unshaven. His suspicions were confirmed by the pungent smell of whiskey that flushed out of the house and exuded from the man.

But it wasn't his neighbor's appearance, or even the odor that burned his eyes and had his attention, it was his identity. He would never forget that face. It had scarred his childhood, and it wasn't until this moment, until this *reunion* that he realized how much. Ken Bailey was the man's name.

A warmth encased his insides and his vision grew clearer.

"Freak, what the fuck is up?" Ken leaned against the doorframe but lost his mark and stumbled to regain his balance.

This arrogant son of a bitch didn't recognize him. It provided him clarity—and strength. A shiver laced down his spine as he stepped inside the house.

"Hey!" Ken slammed a hand against his shoulder.

It shuffled him back a few feet, but he never lost his balance. He was sober as a priest, thanks to Ken interrupting his evening's plans.

He pushed past Ken into the house. He shut the door behind him and stood there, facing his opponent, breathing as if he'd run a marathon. His heart beat so fast, it pained in his chest. Whatever happened next, Ken would deserve it for what he had done to her.

"Get out of my hou—"

He felt cartilage shift under the impact of his fist to Ken's nose.

Ken instinctively cradled his nose and blood poured down his face. A red mist spewed from his mouth as he spoke. "What the—"

"It's your past calling, asshole."

He landed another blow. Ken's nose was broken.

Still, Ken retaliated, coming at him with force, and pinned him to the back of the door. It knocked the wind out of him.

He doubled in half, clenching at his injured abdomen, his eyes only seeing one color—red.

At that moment, adrenaline fused through his system, cording his sinew into tight springs ready to pounce. He would make him pay, make him beg for his next breath. He would no longer be viewed as weak and puny, instead, as powerful and in control.

He thrust his fist toward Ken's jaw but missed when he diverted to the side and dipped low. He took aim again, but a blow to his face stopped all movement.

White, searing pain hindered his vision. A constant rhythm pumped in his head, the music now a deadened cacophony.

Ken stood across from him, winded, each exhale exuding alcohol blended with nicotine.

"You don't even know who I am, do you?"

"I don't need to know you to kill you." The man charged at him, the motive clear.

He had mere seconds, if not merely *a* second, to assess his surroundings and calculate the odds. They were in the kitchen. Dishes were piled on the counters and in the sink. Empty beer bottles covered the table. On the floor next to them were, easily, twenty to thirty alcohol magnums waiting to be returned for a refund.

He ducked just in time.

Ken's fist met with the wood door and had him howling in pain—but not for long. He came at him again, wrapped his hands around his middle and worked to pull him to a straight position. "You think you can come in here and attack me!"

The jab met his cheek, sliding his jaw askew and sinking his teeth into his tongue. He tasted blood.

He glanced back to the bottles again. They were close enough that he could…

Ken yanked on his coat and pulled him upright. His opponent threw a punch and he returned one. They continued to come at each other, both men juking to avoid the other's blows, the odd one making purchase.

It was a misstep that had his foot twisting at a precarious angle, the move to divert, working to his detriment. He fell. Hard. He scrambled to regain equal footing.

It was too late. Ken came down on top of him with powerful force, straddling his mid-section and constricting his airflow.

The music came back into focus. The droning guitar and screaming singer.

The blows landed consecutively, meeting with his face, his shoulders, his gut, and his sides until Ken paused, panting, and looked down at him.

"Now I know who you are." Still mounted over him, his laughter shrilled above the noise disguised as music. "I recognize your shriveling nature." More mocking laughter. Ken was driven to tears with his amusement.

He saw the one color again. Did he have what it took to take a man's life? He used to be peaceful…until he was eight and this man stripped his innocence. Life *wasn't* but a dream, sweetheart.

He bucked, trying to break his arm free, but Ken applied more pressure.

It was time. He had a decision to make. Would he continue to loll back and let the Baileys of the world overpower him forever? Or would he make it clear, once and for all time, that he wasn't a man to be fucked with?

His insides warmed. His extremities cooled.

He assessed the bottles that were beside his head and he figured out what he had to do. But did he have the guts to do it? He had come over here prepared to fight, hadn't he? Well, he found one. He just hadn't expected it to be with Ken Bailey.

But what real difference did it make? It only reinforced the direction and power of Fate. He had been brought to this point in his life for a reason. He was tired of letting everyone down—especially himself.

His fingertips grazed the edge of the closest bottle—a clear rum bottle. His fingers danced across the glass until he had a hold on it.

The hyena laughter stopped. Ken came to, realizing the intention in his eyes.

Ken drew his arm back to make a fatal blow—it was too late.

"For Molly, you asshole!" He let out a roar that challenged the music and ripped the bottle from the floor. He would be the last thing this man would see.

He wailed against him with the bottle until, finally, the glass weakened and shattered, raining over him, to reveal jagged edges.

Minutes later, he hoisted the lifeless body of Ken Bailey, off of him and onto the floor.

His legs were rubbery when he went to stand, but he had proven himself. He had stood up to the bully and had come out the victor.

He gazed down and noticed Bailey's chest still rose softly. Scanning the room, he found the perfect thing to fix that.

When he was finished, he decided he had something to celebrate after all.

CHAPTER 1

THE PLANE TOUCHED DOWN AT Denver International Airport just after six in the morning. I was happy to have the tumultuous flight over with and thought it should have been canceled, but apparently those responsible for that sort of thing had cleared take-off.

Flying typically didn't bother me, but high winds and various temperature pockets had buffeted the plane, rocking it almost like a ship at sea, only we were thirty thousand feet in the air. Land never looked so good.

Zachery slapped me on the back and had me lurching forward from the momentum. "We made it, Pending."

Months into my probationary period but still not clear of it—something I was reminded of all the time by his beloved nickname.

Jack brushed past, leading the three of us through the airport, no doubt driven by the undying urge for a cigarette. Paige hung back, and when I turned, she pushed a rogue strand of hair from her eyes and dipped to the left as she shifted the position of her suitcase strap on her right shoulder.

We were called to Colorado because some old-timer detective by the name of Mack McClellan was confident the area had a serial killer. He believed it strongly enough we were convinced as well.

The label *serial killer* no longer fazed me, and it only took a few horrid cases to rub off its shock value.

Regular people, who didn't have to hunt down murderers, lived life as if they were merely characters fabricated for entertainment purposes. The dark truth was, conservatively, there were an estimated thirty-five to fifty serial killers in the United States at any given time.

The local FBI office was to provide us with transportation, but it was the local detective who insisted on meeting us at the airport and bringing us up to speed.

Stepping out of the warm cocoon of the airport into the brisk winter air of Denver stole my breath. It had me wanting to retreat back inside for the warm, blowing vents.

For recreational purposes, Denver would be an ideal location to spend the Christmas season, with its mountain slopes and deep snow. Even facing the search for a killer, I'd rather be here, miles away from home, than facing the emptiness of the house on Christmas day.

This would be the first year without Deb. The only thing that could make it better was reconciliation, but we were beyond that point. Truth be told, I wasn't even sure if I'd take her back. The divorce was already filed, and knowing my penchant for attracting negative events, it would be official in time for the holiday. It didn't matter though. I had found a way to move forward in my life—at least I told myself that. Maybe I was burying my feelings, but I preferred to think I healed faster than most.

"Hey, there they are."

A man pushed off the hood of a Crown Vic, the cup in his hand steaming in the cold air. At full height, he was all of five eight. His hair was sparse and reminded me of a Chia Pet just starting to grow, but what he did have was a dark blond. He wore a thigh-length wool parka, zipped up shy of his collar by about six inches. It revealed a white collared shirt and a blue tie with white dots. I wondered if he dressed this way all the time or only when the FBI was in town.

He put his cup on the car roof and came toward us with another man who wore a fur-lined leather jacket paired with blue jeans, which appeared stiff due to the mountain air.

It had me wondering which scenario was more uncomfortable,

frozen stiff jeans or breezy dress pants. I experienced the latter and questioned the wardrobe I had brought, wondering if I'd be warm enough.

Curse winter and all that's white.

"Gentleman, I'm Mack McClellan." The man in the parka extended his hand, first to Jack. He must have sensed his authority despite the lit cigarette.

Jack took a quick inhale and blew a stream of white pollution out the side of his mouth as he shook the man's hand. "Supervisory Special Agent Jack Harper and this is my team." Jack left us to introduce ourselves.

McClellan's gaze settled on me, and I surmised what he was thinking—I was the young guy on the team, the inexperienced one he'd have to watch.

He gestured to the man with him. "This is Detective Ronnie Hogan. He's also with Denver PD. We're not partners, but he's of the same mind. There's a serial at play here."

Hogan bobbed his head forward as a greeting but made no effort to extend a hand. His eyes were brown and hard to read. Crease lines etched in his brow, but he also had smile lines, so there was some promise there. Not that we witnessed the expression.

McClellan grinned with a warmth that touched his eyes, giving me the impression he was used to Hogan's aloofness. "Glad to see you made it all right. It's quite the weather we're having these days. How was your flight?"

Jack took another drag on his cigarette. "Over now."

His retort killed the expression on the detective's face. "A man who is all business, I see. So, the dead body. You know the name and details."

Another pull on the cigarette and Jack flicked the glowing butt to the ground and extinguished it with the twist of a shoe.

"We know what the file says, but we like to go over everything in person." Paige smiled at the detectives, no doubt trying to compensate for Jack's crass behavior.

"Well, let us fill you in on the way to where the body was found. My, it's mighty cold out here." He rubbed his hands together and grabbed his cup before going around to the driver's side. "For everyone to be more comfortable, two of you can come with me, and the other two can go with Hogan."

McClellan seemed like an open book—what you saw was what you got. With Hogan, there was something about him, whether it was his skepticism or what, I wasn't sure. A quality that should repel actually made me want to get to know him.

"I'll go with Hogan." Paige and I spoke at the same time.

Our eyes connected. In the past this symmetry in thought would have elicited a smile from both of us. These days our relationship was more complicated.

Paige stepped back and sought Jack's direction. "I'll go with whoever you want me to."

"It's fine. You guys go with Hogan. We'll all catch up at the crime scene."

She went past me and held out her hand to Hogan. "I don't think we've been properly introduced."

Hogan stared at her extended hand and, eventually, conceded to a handshake. The greeting was over quick.

As he was getting into the driver's seat, I whispered in Paige's ear. "He's not really the touchy-feely kind, is he?"

I received a glare in response.

CHAPTER 2

"THINGS MUST BE SLOW FOR you guys if you're willing to come all the way here for this case." Hogan kept his eyes on the road, his voice level as he spoke. He made a quick pass of a slower-moving vehicle.

My fingers gripped the armrest on the door, indenting the foam beneath it. "You're not buying that it's a serial at work?"

A small snort, which could have been construed as a laugh. "I'm not saying anything. McClellan can be a convincing man. I agree the situations surrounding these men are similar. Whether that means anything more, I haven't fully decided."

He touched the brakes, and the back end of the car lost traction and swayed to the right. No one else seemed to notice or care.

"How long have you been with Denver PD?" Paige asked.

It warranted a quick, sideways glance from Hogan. "Is this where you try to get to know me better?"

Paige's jaw tightened. "If you don't like people, why are you a cop?"

I settled into the seat, happy that I wasn't on the receiving end for a change. Part of me wished to be elsewhere, the other part wondered who would come out the victor.

"Who says I don't like people? I like people. I just don't like feds."

"And what have we done to you?"

Hogan kept his eyes straight ahead. "McClellan feels the latest victim was left there for us to find. Like this guy wants to get caught."

"So that's how you get by in life? You shut people down who try to get close."

"You want to get close to me, sweetheart, we'll do it after hours, but now's the job."

Air rushed from Paige's mouth, skimming over teeth and making a *whooshing* sound on the exhale. She knotted her arms and kicked her back into the seat as she did so.

Hogan didn't give any indication he was affected by her response. He took a street on the right, made a quick left, parked, and cut the engine. "We're here."

"I'm glad you told us," Paige mumbled and got out of the car.

We had beat the other detective and the rest of our team, but as we made our way toward the dumpster, the department-issued sedan pulled in, crunching snow beneath the wheels.

When we were all standing around the dumpster at the back of Lynn's Bakery, McClellan pointed to the right of the bin.

"The body was found right there. He was covered in snow, with only the tip of his boots showing. The waste removal company found him when they came to empty the bin. At first they thought someone was too lazy to pick up the trash and dispose of it properly. They stepped out to lift it and got more than they expected."

"Something that they even got out of the vehicle. Most would carry on and not care. They're hired to empty the container, not clean up the surrounding area," Paige said.

"Exactly what I thought."

"Did you question the garbage man?"

"Yeah. Even pulled a background. Nothing came of it."

"Name's Craig Bowen," Zachery interjected.

McClellan seemed impressed by Zachery. "Read that in the file? Good memory. The cause of death?"

"Rat poison."

The man had no idea with whom he was dealing.

"Impressive. Now this guy didn't go silently, or easily, that's for sure."

"And you think this is connected to animal cruelty cases?" I asked the question to get things moving forward.

"Yes, I do. The vic's name was Darren Simpson. Twenty-six years ago he was charged with feeding his dog rat poison, but the charges didn't stick. The guy walked. It was big news around here."

"Animal cruelty cases are big news?"

"Well, there's a spot for them in the paper. Bigger news years ago than it is these days."

"So this guy was accused of poisoning animals twenty-six years ago and you think someone's coming back for revenge now?" Paige asked.

"Exactly what I'm thinking."

Hogan rolled his eyes.

I gestured to him and addressed McClellan. "Your friend here doesn't seem convinced."

McClellan smirked. "Nothing much fazes Hogan, but he does concede to the line of thought that *something* is going on here."

"The file mentions there are a few missing men, and this is why you're convinced there's a serial killer," Zachery said.

"Yes. Two date back a bit ago. Dean Garner went missing in two thousand nine. Charges against him were microwaving a Chihuahua. They were dropped because there wasn't enough evidence. Karl Ball was charged with pit-bull fighting but got off on a technicality. He went missing in two thousand ten."

"So, our victim poisoned his dog and then dies of poisoning," I made the summation. "It certainly sounds like more than a coincidence."

"Our unsub is targeting animal abusers who beat the charges. He carries out his own sort of vigilante justice, bringing the same punishment upon them as they inflicted," Zachery said.

Paige tossed some hair behind her shoulder. "Is it wrong to side with a killer in this case? What kind of monster abuses animals? They rely on us for protection, for food, for shelter, for love, and how are they repaid? Abuse. The thought makes *me* angry enough to kill."

"He?" McClellan picked up on Zachery's reference to gender. He rested his hands on his hips and drummed his fingers there.

"It's a logical deduction to presume the killer we seek is male. The targeted victims are men for one," Zachery explained.

"But poison? Isn't that a common method for females?"

"It is, however, no women that fit the profile of being animal abusers are missing, are they?"

"No."

"That lends it toward being a man hunting other men."

Hogan stepped toward Paige. "All I know is this guy needs to be stopped. These are people he's killing, not animals."

Paige's jaw jutted up. "You sure?"

"I agree they were charged with barbaric acts, but they deserve to be heard and have a fair trial."

"Guess you do like people." Paige secured eye contact with Hogan. He turned away first.

Jack slipped a hand into his coat pocket. "While the background is good to have, the real reason we're here is because you feel the threat is still viable, and you convinced us of that. What really got our attention was the recently missing man."

McClellan nodded. "His name is Gene Lyons. His wife reported him five days ago, but after Simpson, we realized the similarities. He was charged with animal neglect, resulting in a beagle barely hanging onto life. They nursed him back at significant expense, only to find out, in the end, the dog's mind had snapped. They had to put him down. The charge against Lyons was made twenty-five years ago."

Anger ripped through me. The man we hunted—was he a monster or a hero? What sane human being wouldn't consider, even with a passing thought, the execution of revenge on those who abused animals? This case would be a tough one.

"The file said that all four men were married," Zachery said. "Four, including Simpson, our murdered victim."

A slow nod from McClellan. "Not all happily, but in somewhat committed relationships."

"Did you speak with them?" Jack asked.

McClellan answered. "Oh yeah. Let's just say the women in these men's lives are interesting. We'll leave it at that. They had alibis if you want to call them that. Of course, you say you're looking for a man...but the strongest defense was Simpson's wife, who was spending the night in jail for a drunk and disorderly. Let's just say some people dance to the beat of a different drummer. These would be them."

"The file said Garner's wife, Jill, was home watching TV when she decided enough time had passed and her husband should be home. Ball's wife, Renee, was out drinking with her girlfriends at the time of his disappearance." Zachery burrowed his hands into his coat pockets. "With Lyons, the wife was trying to hunt him down for some spending money and couldn't find him. She didn't really know exactly when he went missing."

"Correct on all counts. Lyons and his wife were separated but making it work like that. They led separate lives, except when it came to finances. He carried her."

"His line of work?"

"A computer geek."

"You've got to be kidding me. Just when you'd think he'd be harmless, he's at home abusing the dog." Paige bounced, in what appeared to be an effort to fend off the cold.

"Why don't we go inside Lynn's? She's got hot coffee and baked goods you would die for. Besides, there's no sense us standing outside and freezing."

"Sounds good to me." Paige smiled.

Jack nodded and the team followed the local detectives.

LYNN'S BAKERY WAS A FAMILY-RUN BUSINESS. It hadn't been touched by corporate America with their flashy monikers that signified a franchise. Stepping inside, the warmth made my cheeks tingle and encased me in a metaphorical hug while the smell of cinnamon buns and apple pie baking in the oven tantalized.

In a front display case, there was an assortment of baked goods, which included cookies, muffins, scones, donuts, pastries, and cakes. Everything came in a seemingly endless variety. On the counter were more tiered confections, with slices missing, displayed in glass domes. A wooden easel held a chalkboard sign that read *Please seat yourself.*

We followed its direction and pushed two tables together.

McClellan gestured to a waitress. She was maybe twenty and had long brown hair that was swept back into a loose ponytail, with the exception of two curly strands that dangled in front of each ear. Her eyes were pale green and she didn't wear any makeup. Stitched onto her uniform was the name, *Annie*. She held a pen in her left hand and a small notepad in her right.

"You guys all here 'cause of—" She gestured with the end of the pen behind her shoulder, denoting the back alley.

"Now, what have I told you, Annie?" Detective McClellan sustained eye contact with her.

"Dad, I'm just curious. It's not a big deal. You guys are all FBI?" She smiled at me.

Paige didn't miss the attention I received and raised her brow.

"We're here to warm up, not to meet and greet," McClellan directed her.

Annie's shoulders sagged and her hips jutted to the right. "Fine."

"All right, so we'll each have a coffee and a Christmas special cookie."

Annie's pen never met paper and she walked away. I was left wondering a couple things, one being, what was a "*Christmas special cookie?*"

I voiced my other observation. "You never told us your daughter worked here."

McClellan waved a dismissive hand. "What does it really matter? She didn't kill that man."

"That you know of."

"You're serious? I thought you said that it was a—"

I smiled at the detective.

He grimaced in return and rested his hand on a napkin. He fanned up its edge and repeated the cycle a few times. "As we were starting to discuss out—"

Annie put a coffee in front of Jack. "You must be the boss. It's easy to tell."

Did I deduct an underlying smile from Jack?

"I am." He reached for a sugar packet from a small glass bowl in the middle of the table.

She set the tray down with the rest of our coffees and extended a hand to Jack. "I'm Annie."

He shook her hand. "Jack Harper."

"Annie, we don't have time for this."

Annie ground one of her shoes into the floor. "My Dad likes to control everything I do. He drives me nuts."

"Well, until you pay your own rent."

"Yadda, yadda." She looked at me. "You ever get the as-long-as-you-live-under-my-roof speech from your parents?"

How young did she think I was? I had at least seven or eight years on her.

"You're kidding? He still gets that." Zachery, who was sitting beside me, patted my back.

Annie laughed. The expression suited her—well. She was probably a heartbreaker. I had a feeling McClellan was well aware of it too. His attention narrowed in on me.

"Annie, please, we have work to do."

She rolled her eyes and distributed the coffees, then held the round tray against her chest when she was finished. "If it's true that murdered man killed a dog, then he deserved what he got." Annie gauged us for a response, but when none of us offered one, she left.

"You discuss open cases with your daughter?" Jack asked.

"I didn't discuss anything with her. The news was all over it."

"The news?"

"You know what they're like. They sniff out murder like ants do a picnic."

"Hmm."

"We were talking about the missing men's significant others," Paige interjected, "before we came inside. Tell us more about them."

McClellan pulled his eyes from Jack. "None of the women have a violent history. Even with Simpson's drunk and disorderly, she wasn't hostile, she was half-naked in a public place. Charges of indecent exposure should have been pursued."

"Why weren't they? You said she spent the night in jail."

Color saturated the detective's face. "That's all she got. The chief thought formal charges were excessive."

"She is a nice-looking piece of ass." Jack pulled out his pack of cigarettes and placed it on the table. His hand covered it, but he didn't light up. There were no smoking signs posted all over.

"Yeah."

"What about here? Anything about this site that seems significant?" I asked.

McClellan shook his head. "None that we're aware of at this point."

"We need to know who wrote the articles on all of these men. We need to speak to the garbage man who found Simpson, his significant other, along with those of the other missing men," Jack addressed his team. "I'd say things possibly started with Karl Ball, who went missing in two thousand and nine, but we've got a fresh body and a new missing persons case. We dig into those first."

"Agree, Boss." Paige blew on her coffee and took a sip.

"I believe we're after a male killer who targets those who specifically abuse dogs." I offered a summation.

Zachery popped a piece of cookie into his mouth and jabbed the uneaten part toward me. "Good point. He probably also experienced something at a younger age that made him predisposed to—"

Hogan coughed and held a hand over his mouth. Its source, clearly, was derision.

We all looked at him.

"You can tell all of this from what we have so far?"

"Hogan, please." McClellan leaned into his chair and flung his arm over the back.

"It just seems like, what's the point of local law enforcement as long as we have the FBI." He tossed a five on the table and stood.

McClellan shot to his feet and leaned in toward Hogan. He spoke low, but it was easy to hear. "Why are you acting like this? You said you'd be of help."

Hogan scanned McClellan's face but addressed us. "I want this killer stopped just as much as all of you, but a serial at work? Unsub? Your fancy terminology for what we would call a perp. You have to do everything different. And, if that's not enough, you have to pry your nose into our cases." Back to McClellan. "I've gotta go do some police work." He left, and his wet boots squeaked across the floor of the bakery.

McClellan's inhale expanded his chest. He took his seat again. "I'm sorry about him."

"From the file, one journalist reported on all these cases," Zachery said.

"Yeah." McClellan's hand went for his coffee. Disappointment radiated from him, but he tried to counter with a smile. It didn't fully form. "The guy's name is Kent Fields, now a giant in the publishing industry. He's got three Pulitzers to his credit and many other awards. I highly doubt it's him behind these murders."

"He might have information, from behind the scenes, that will prove useful to the investigation."

"You sure about that? Remember these cases go back twenty-six years. That's a long time."

"We'll see if it feels that long ago to him."

Enlightenment dawned on the detective's face. "Ah, so you'll set a trap for the rat. If he bites, he could be our man."

Zachery nodded. "Precisely."

"It might not be a bad idea to talk to the main animal activist group in town either. I'll get you their information."

"There's a lot of people we need to speak with and we're not getting it done sitting around here." Jack stood and the rest of us followed his lead.

"You guys take my car. I'll call for a ride." McClellan's gaze went to the window. Outside large snowflakes fell in quick succession.

"Don't worry, Detective, we get snow in Virginia." Jack slipped out a cigarette and tucked the package back into his pocket.

McClellan's eyes went to it. "Of course you do. I didn't—"

"We'll head to the station first, see if our rides are there, and get someone to come back for you."

"I'd appreciate it."

I can't say that I was excited about Jack driving in this weather. Behind the wheel, the man typically scared me on sunny days, but I hurried, hoping to call shotgun first.

Chapter 3

His hands shook every time, but someone had to clean up the city. The government certainly wasn't going to do anything about it. Those who were elected put on a show for glamor and fame with no real purpose. They slept in their million-dollar homes and shut out the ugliness of the world around them. For appearance's sake, they went to their charity benefits while being too lazy to deal with the issues. The promises made to those who'd voted them into office in the first place were forgotten. It was a disgusting irony that defined politics. The very men who swore to deal with issues, to rectify injustices, sat on the sidelines, more incompetent than most.

This is why he was left to take the power into his own hands and make a difference to society. He brought justice for the Defenseless by condemning their Offender.

It was this reasoning that added justification for his actions. Everyone had a purpose. His was to speak for the victims who have no voice. He was their Advocate.

Placing Simpson's body on display was a message to the world to let them know crimes against the Defenseless would not be tolerated, and that those who inflicted abuse upon them would be held accountable.

This Offender, his latest captive, would take patience, but that was one thing he had developed over the years. A tempering of knowing when best to strike, and whom.

The Advocate watched his captive through a camera he had placed in the man's cell. The Offender was extended the same courtesies he had provided his canine companion—a dank corner with an empty food dish and a shitty water bowl. To complete the retribution, he put a tight choker around his neck and attached it to a short chain.

For hours, the man had protested his captivity, but now his cries for help had lost conviction. What was once a high-pitched fervor had dulled to a mumbled whisper. Despair and hopelessness were taking over.

The thought made the Advocate smile. He was making a difference. He offered no mercy for these men. The Offenders deserved what was coming their way, and if he was the one destined to exact the punishment, he would see it through. Exacting revenge and punishment on these mongrels had become his driving purpose in life. It was what he was meant to do.

The Offender was alternating between balling his fists and pulling out on the choker, but his efforts were futile. The collar was latched tight and secured with a tiny padlock.

"Aw, is it getting a little harder to breathe?" the Advocate said to himself. Laughter had his eyes pinching shut and tears seeping from the corners.

The man kept trying to reach the bench to sit down, but the length of the chain had been adjusted so there was no possibility of that happening. He would stand or hang himself.

Still, the Advocate experienced no remorse. The Offender should have thought through to the consequences of his actions before he outworked his madness on one of the Defenseless.

"Why are you doing this?" the Offender called out.

Rarely did the Advocate respond. They didn't deserve to be heard, to be granted a say. He had tried that in the beginning, but their speeches about their being guileless fell not only on deaf ears, but on a mind forged by retribution.

The Advocate pushed the button that would allow his voice to carry into the room. He wasn't worried about being identified—there would be no escape for an Offender—but he had modified the output anyhow. The speech distortion would toy with their minds even further.

"You brought this on yourself."

"I—" The Offender buried his face in his hands, the muffled sobbing still loud enough to hear.

The crying always reaped the opposite of their desired outcome. Instead of it tugging on the Advocate's humanity, his mind went to the Defenseless, to those who wept internally, in darkness.

"You deserve to die!"

The man slid his hands down his face and sputtered, "I haven't done anything."

"Drink your water, animal." It pained the Advocate to equate this mammal to the four-legged variety. The Defenseless were superior to Offenders in many ways.

The man's legs buckled beneath him, the choker, doing its job, tightened its hold against his larynx. The Offender righted himself and his hands rushed to his throat, where he tugged on the collar without much success.

"Drink!"

"Why are you—" Vomit spewed across the room, splattering some on the camera lens.

The Advocate rubbed his hands, sat back, and swiveled in his chair.

Now things were coming together. The man would break, and when he did, the Advocate would be there to watch him take his final breath.

CHAPTER 4

JACK HAD PAIGE CALL NADIA at head office to request a more in-depth background on both the journalist, Kent Fields, and the garbage man, Craig Bowen.

Nadia Webber was our contact at Quantico, who managed to gather any data we required. Her expertise and know-how contributed toward solving every case.

We reached the police station and two shiny, black SUVs were parked in the lot. Based on the lack of accumulated snow, I surmised they had just recently been dropped off. Our coffee break and discussion weren't a waste of time.

We handed over McClellan's keys and requested that he be picked up at Lynn's Bakery. A few officers heard us mention the name and were eager to volunteer for the task. I have to admit the Christmas cookies would serve as sufficient payment.

After retrieving the keys for the SUVs, we reconvened outside.

Jack lit a cigarette and waved it toward Paige. "I want you and Zach to visit Gene Lyons's wife. Find out when she saw him last, what he was up to. Brandon and I are going to speak with Simpson's wife."

"Figures. You guys get the hot one. Be sure to keep it in your pants, Pending." Zachery laughed.

"Come on." Though what I had with Paige was not exactly a committed relationship, it still had the confines of one. I angled my head to the side, concerned about her reaction.

She was smiling. Her eyes teased. "He does have a point, Brandon."

If she kept acting like that, we'd have a really hard time keeping our attraction from Jack. As it was, we flirted with the edge of insubordination. As members of the same team, there wasn't to be any fraternization. It was too late for that a few times over. And, factoring in the possible repercussions, it was stupid. There was a lot at stake. I was a probationary agent and Jack probably wouldn't have an issue knocking me out of the bureau. Paige faced removal from Jack's team.

I returned her smile, opting to play it light. "Why? Are you going to get jealous, Dawson?"

"Jealous? Of you? Hardly." She laughed, but the spark in her eyes revealed the contradiction.

Jack suctioned in on his cigarette with a definitive *piff*. He was calculating.

"Let's go." I wondered why we gravitated to congregating outdoors when we could have talked in the warmth of the station. Then I realized the blasted cigarette in Jack's hand was to blame.

"Seems someone is eager to get going." It had served as one last jab from Zachery before he walked away with Paige toward their SUV.

FOR THE SECOND TIME THAT day my fingers gripped the armrest and dug into the foam—they alternated between there and the dash. My legs were extended, feet flattened to the floor, pressing on imaginary brakes.

"You do know you have no control over there." Jack tapped his cigarette on his lowered window.

"Even in the frigid arctic, you still need that stick bad enough to let in the cold air."

"This is hardly the Arctic."

I rolled my eyes and faced out the passenger-side window. Another frustrating attempt at conversation with Jack. I might as well go for the gold. During a recent interrogation, he had let something slip and I was determined to get full disclosure. "You never told me about your kids."

He inhaled and flicked the butt out the window, closed it and continued to drive, with his eyes on the road.

According to the GPS we were still twenty minutes out, but the technology didn't account for treacherous roads and weather conditions. Maybe we'd sit in silence the entire way.

When Jack still hadn't responded a minute later, I tried another tactic. "You think I'm going to give up, but I'm not. I'm going to find out—"

Jack faced me.

I peeled one hand off the dash and pointed ahead. "The road."

He ignored my plea. His eyes were still on me. "You want to know about my kid?"

Faced with the direct question, under his burning gaze, I wasn't sure if I cared anymore—and the road conditions...his focus should be there.

If I didn't calm myself and carry out what I had started, he'd never comply. Both my hands went to the dash, but it was freezing. I pulled them back and blew on them, doing my best to be nonchalant. "Only if you want to tell me."

"Hmm."

His eyes went back to the road, and I drew a full breath.

Seconds passed in silence.

"Why not just pull my background?" Jack asked.

"You're kidding."

"Nope."

"I'd need a reason—and clearance."

"You could have Nadia do it."

The gears in my head moved. What could I say to that? That I'd thought about it but would never dream of following through?

"Of course, if I found out you did, you'd be off the team faster than a shooting star."

We slid to a stop at a four-way. To hell with it. I'd brave the cold plastic. "I never have...pulled your background."

"Good."

The GPS showed one minute from our destination. Why did I have a feeling we'd get there and I still wouldn't have an answer?

"You know it doesn't really matter if you have a kid." I shook my head. "Really. It changes nothing." *Just adds a little character…*

"I don't have a kid."

He pulled into the Simpsons' driveway.

"What do you mean? You told that guy months ago—"

"Yeah, I know what I said."

I studied Jack's profile. The intensity of his gaze, how he now avoided eye contact, he was lying.

THE HOUSE WAS IN A NICE NEIGHBORHOOD. I imagined all the lawns would be manicured in the summer months and the garden beds alive with color. The structure itself was gray block, lending it a modernistic design perfect for the architectural types. The front face of the building was broken up by numerous large windows that would let in natural light. Today, there wasn't much of it; the sky was thick with cloud cover. There was only a faint hope that the snow would stop falling anytime soon.

I rang the doorbell and it chimed a beautiful rendition of some classical song I recognized but couldn't name. That wasn't within my realm of expertise, but I'd say the bell had been custom-designed.

A brunette, obviously struggling on her tiptoes, peeked through the high window in the door. Her eyes scanned us from head to as far down as she could see. She lifted a hand and waved us away. "We have religion."

She was still in the window when Jack hit the doorbell again.

The door *whooshed* open, fighting against its seal.

"I told you—" Her attention went to Jack's credentials.

"Can we come in?"

She slid her bottom lip through her teeth. "Sure."

"We want to speak with—"

"Jenna," the brunette yelled over her shoulder. "The FBI is here to see you."

"The FBI?" She pranced, in bare feet, into the grand foyer. When she saw us, her steps slowed.

Jenna Simpson was slight, like the woman who had let us in. She wore tights and an oversized sweater that fell off her right shoulder and exposed the strap of a teal tank top. Based on appearance and genetic structure, the women were not related but merely friends. Jenna had a quality that made men take notice, though. It was hard to ascertain whether it was her physique—which had the necessary female curves—the platinum blond hair or the tastefully applied eye makeup that made her gray eyes appear mysterious. Her cheeks held a healthy glow.

"They're with the FBI." The brunette turned to Jenna.

"I heard you." Jenna laced her arms and addressed us. "What do you want?" The tip of her tongue peeked through her lips.

"Your husband was murdered," Jack said.

Just when I thought he couldn't possibly be any blunter in his phrasing, he managed to surpass my expectations.

"I'm fully aware of that." Her eyelashes fluttered, but she stood her ground.

"Do you have somewhere we can sit and talk?" I asked, doing my best to add a little more delicacy to the situation.

"I'll put on some tea," the brunette said.

Jenna placed a hand on her friend's forearm. "They won't be here for long."

Jenna's eyes disclosed that she was a tangled mess. She was a complicated woman, who many might perceive as less intelligent, given her favorable genetics.

"Remove your shoes and follow me." She hooked her finger and spun on her heels.

I noticed her pedicure matched her french-manicured fingernails.

She led us to a sunken living room. I took in the lavish space, wondering what it would be like to actually live in a place like this. It must make one feel as if they were royalty. Maybe it was immersion in that emotion that bred entitlement and arrogance.

The floor-to-ceiling windows contributed a sense of enchantment and awe. Outside, the snowflakes appeared to be getting larger. "You have a beautiful home."

"Thank you." She smiled—the expression carrying the hint of seduction.

"You're welcome." I would be strong, or Paige would kill me. I broke eye contact and looked at Jack.

He dropped onto a cream colored leather sofa, utilizing the edge of the seat cushion and not getting too comfortable. I sat beside him and took full advantage of the plush hug.

Jenna's eyebrows jabbed upward. "I see this is good cop, bad cop."

I found it interesting that, for a woman who recently lost her husband, she didn't give the impression she was overly affected by his death.

I unzipped my jacket but left it on. The heat of the home had sweat gathering at the nape of my neck and trickling down my back. Even the marble floors were heated, which also explained Jenna's bare feet. Unexpectedly, with the thought, I couldn't picture the woman in socks. She fit better with the imagery of a lingerie model—in high heels and silk.

"Tell us about your husband." Jack's voice sliced through my fantasy.

Jenna peeled her focus from me and cast her gaze to Jack.

Her friend took a seat beside her, and her chestnut eyes narrowed in on me, harboring a glare.

I tugged down on the sleeve of my shirt, which was riding up inside the arm of the jacket.

The brunette rolled her eyes.

Jenna crossed her legs, away from her friend, toward me. "What do you want to know?"

"Did he have any enemies?"

"It's a typical question I'm sure you get sick of asking, but no. Not that I know of. I mean, who wouldn't love him?" She spread her arms to take in the room. "The man was loaded. Even if people didn't like him, you'd never know. They'd smile and wish him a good day. Know what I mean?" She hitched an eyebrow again.

"What did he do for work?"

Another smile. "You should know that from some file, shouldn't you? Surely there's more valuable information that I could provide to you."

I faced Jack, but his profile held steady, his gaze settled on her. I wondered if he registered her good looks, or whether he remained oblivious. Part of me hoped he was aware. He was still a man. The other part of me wouldn't be surprised if he were ignorant of the fact she was a beauty. He tended to lean more toward business than pleasure.

"There was quite an age difference between you," Jack said.

"I prefer a mature man, and we made it work."

"Did you?"

"Are you accusing me of killing him?"

"You don't seem very upset?"

A bolt flashed across her eyes. "Would it work better for you if I were in a white, fluffy robe with matching slippers, had a puffy face and a red-tipped nose? If tissues were coming out of pockets because they couldn't possibly hold anymore?" She simpered and sank further into the couch. "Please."

This chick was cold as ice.

"You 'made it work?' Those were your words. You don't sound like you were happy."

She rolled her eyes, dramatically, and accompanied the motion with a rushed exhale. "We were okay. All right? Is that what you want to hear?"

The brunette shot to her feet. "I'm not sure why you're pushing her like this. Do you think she killed him?"

I held up a hand to encourage her to take a seat again. She disregarded the gesture, but it didn't stop me from saying my bit. "We're not accusing her of anything, but if we can get some straightforward answers, we'll be out of your way, and you both can get on with your day."

She dropped back onto the couch.

Jenna's steel gaze went to me. "You want to know if he had enemies? Yes. Don't ask me for a list though."

Since Jenna seemed more inclined to talk to me than she did to Jack, I carried on. "Were any of these people angered because of what he did to his dog?"

Her composure faltered and had her going pale for a fraction of a second. "I suppose so. I wasn't around then, but if they were, they had no right to be." She shrugged. "There wasn't proof he did it."

"The dish with Warfarin—that's rat poison—and a bowl of antifreeze were pulled from this house. Is the house not in his name?"

Jenna hugged herself briefly and afterward tucked her hands under her thighs. "He didn't do it."

"Then who did?"

The house went silent as a tomb. There wasn't even the ticking of a clock or the humming of a furnace.

"Listen, the charges didn't stick, and what was that—twenty-some years ago? Some sicko targeted him after this long?" Stress tore at Jenna's facial features, giving her hard lines. "I honestly believe that his bitchy of a wife at the time did it. I really do. That woman is a nut job."

With her words, I remembered reading that she was his second wife in the file. Somehow I had forgotten, probably due to the fact my mind was a cluttered mess from my personal life.

She angled her head to the left. "I took him from her. She didn't deserve him."

"You were his secretary." The pieces were filling in.

"Yes. I noticed you didn't phrase that one as a question. You know what he did for work. I love how cops know the answers but still ask. He ran Simpson Construction. He made it from the ground up. He didn't stand on his parents' legacy. He created one." Passion ignited in her eyes. "He was a believer in dreams, but he—" Her voice went gravelly and tears filled her eyes. "He made them come true."

The brunette wrapped her arm around Jenna, and Jenna leaned into the embrace.

I didn't dare verbalize the thought, but it was apparent she'd loved Darren Simpson. The bravado presented was simply that, a façade.

"This person, the one who did this—" Jenna's chin quivered and tears ran down her cheeks. "Was a sick son of a bitch. Darren didn't deserve this."

I was left speechless and somehow managed to keep my opinion to myself. This case was one of deep-seated conflict. The abused animals were given voice by the killer extracting vigilante justice, but on the flipside, our unsub was killing men and taking the stand as judge, jury, and executioner. The death sentence wasn't even legal punishment in many states.

"You said he had people who didn't like him. Anyone new in his life?"

"Not that I know of."

The brunette straightened up. "What about that guy he mentioned?"

"Guy?"

"Yeah, you've been complaining about Darren spending more time away from you."

"Oh, it's nothing, Emily."

I inched forward on the sofa. "Jenna, it could be something."

Her eyes pinched and her brow wrinkled as if a twinge of pain caught her unexpectedly. "You think he could be connected to Darren's death somehow?"

"It's possible. Everything helps to get us closer."

"I don't know his name. Gawd!" She put a flattened palm to her forehead and faced the ceiling. "I should have listened more when he spoke. I'm such a bad listener."

"Do you know what he looked like?"

"No. I'm sorry." As her eyes connected with mine, they crackled with revelation. "They'd go to a bar named Smitty's and play pool."

CHAPTER 5

PAIGE HATED THE JEALOUSY THAT thrived beneath the surface. She'd never experienced any of these emotions prior to Brandon. She even remembered feeling lonely, years ago, when he had left the academy and returned to his wife. She should have known things would come full circle and she'd have to face the consequences of getting involved with a married agent in training. She just didn't realize how cruel, and ironic, Karma could be in pairing them on the same team with the BAU. Her peace had come with convincing herself she didn't need to worry about seeing him again. She was in New York, he lived in Florida. What were the chances their paths would ever cross again? But life wasn't always fair. In fact, most times, reality was cruel. It had a way of serving notices that made most people stand back and analyze their life—where they were and where they were headed, what they regretted and how to make things better. It was one certainty she was convinced would never change.

She and Zach were on their way to visit Gene Lyons's wife, and, even though, her mind should have been on the case, it kept straying to the sidelines. Maybe she should resign? If she couldn't gather her thoughts and focus, what good was she doing?

She shuffled the internal monolog and told herself it wasn't Brandon, it was the time of year.

She glanced over at Zach's profile. His attention was steadied on the road and the slippery conditions. The snow kept falling.

"Is Christmas a big deal for you?" she asked.

He didn't take his eyes off the road. "Not a huge deal. Maybe more so for my mom. You?"

"Huge, and I love everything about it."

"You know it's of pagan origins and dates back to three fifty-four AD?"

"Please don't take something beautiful and destroy it."

"I'm just telling you, it's not the glitter and glam it's made out to be."

She paused to smile wistfully, letting her mind wander. She conjured the smell of gingerbread, evergreen, and eggnog. She could hear the crackling of a fire in the fireplace. "But it brings people together. Everyone is different at this time of year."

"They are different all right, more consumed with commercialism."

"Zach."

He snuck in a quick glance and grinned at her. "I can't help it sometimes."

"Uh-huh."

"You say you love everything?"

"Getting gifts, giving gifts. The lights, how they sparkle."

"I noticed the order."

She laughed. "I'm still a woman, Zach."

"You're sad you might miss it?"

Faced with the direct question, it stirred up a lot of emotion. She hated that it centered on Brandon. She wanted him to be a part of the festivities this year, but she sensed that life would take another turn.

"You know, even if we haven't closed the case, we can celebrate here."

"What? In a local restaurant or our hotel?" She sulked.

"Well, it wouldn't be exactly the same, but you'd be with us. Just think, it will probably be a lot less drama than other years."

Her thoughts skipped to last Christmas. Her younger sister had gotten into a fight with their mother over what stuffing recipe to use. She thought about her uncle who was always too close to the family, not in a creepy sort of way, but still, he had never married and integrated himself as if he were an immediate relative.

She bobbed her head side to side. "True." She recognized her tone carried a playful edge, but inside she was torn. Part of her had wanted to invite Brandon to celebrate with the Dawson family. Would he even accept if she extended the offer?

Zach pulled to the curb in front of a bungalow. The barrage of snow had been left to accumulate in the driveway and was nearing twenty inches deep. If it wasn't for the mound in the shape of a car, and the lights on inside the house, Paige would have guessed no one was home.

"You're telling me we have to walk through all that—"

"Merry Christmas."

"Zach, I could beat you right now."

"I ALWAYS TOLD HIM, Karma's a bitch and she will collect one day. He thought I was talking about myself." Cathy Lyons sat in a sofa chair, her legs up on its matching ottoman, underneath a blanket. Her dog, Biscuit, a Pomeranian, snuggled tightly against her and shifted his position whenever she moved.

The house was a disorganized mess. Empty alcohol bottles were in the front entry, as if soldiers lined up on the battlefield, only they had lost the fight. Dog hair was meshed together in clumps on the ceramic tile and blew as tumbleweeds in the wake of following her to the living room.

When Paige took a seat on the sofa, the overwhelming scent of dog rushed up, tickling her nose. She didn't have time to stop the sneeze. "Excuse me." Tears whelmed in Paige's eyes, but she blinked them back. "It's safe to say you two didn't exactly get along."

"Oh no, but we had an arrangement."

"An arrangement?"

"He lived his life, I lived mine."

"It had always been that way?" Zach asked.

Cathy angled her head and pulled back. "Most couples get married because they love each other, they can even stand each other. His gambling killed us."

"Why not get a divorce?"

Cathy's face contorted, mimicking a squished raisin. "That

would be a sin."

Paige studied the woman. She never understood why people fought to hold a relationship together when it had run its course. Drawing comparison to her own situation, the thought turned her stomach.

"You reported him missing five days ago." Zach attempted to realign the direction of the conversation.

"That I did. The cops didn't even seem to care until that guy's body showed up." She *tsked* and shook her head. "Found in a back alley, poisoned to death. I read the paper." For some reason, her latter statement carried pride.

Paige's thoughts went to Gene Lyons. Here, a man who'd been accused of animal neglect, still had the decency to remain married to and support his bride—a woman for whom he surely couldn't have had any respect. Did he do it out of love, or out of obligation? Contrast that to what he was accused of doing—hurting an innocent animal—it wasn't aligning.

"Were you both free to see other people?" Paige asked.

"Absolutely. We were just not allowed to live with anyone of the opposite sex. That would be a sin."

Cohabiting was a sin but conjugating wasn't. Interesting. This woman had the ability to perverse the marital bonds and make it esthetic.

Zach crossed his leg, letting his ankle rest on the knee of the other. "The report says you filed a missing persons report when he didn't show up to drop off your money."

"Yes."

"He typically did so reliably?"

"Yes."

Zach turned to Paige. He must have sensed her amusement with this scenario. She couldn't understand why the guy would have put up with this woman, married or not.

"You were living together at the time he was charged with animal neglect?"

"Yes."

Zach's chest expanded. "Did you think he was guilty?"

"Yes."

Zach dropped his leg. "Did you voice that at the time?"

"What good would it have done?"

Paige was happy that she'd responded with more than a fired-back *Yes*.

"Your husband is missing and we suspect that he's been targeted by the same person who killed Darren Simpson."

Her brows knit together.

"The man found by the dumpster," Zach led her.

Recognition lit in her eyes. "Yes, I read that."

Paige covered her mouth to stifle the snicker but dropped her hand under Zach's gaze.

"You really believe he's been kidnaped by a killer?" Fascination carried over each word and her posture had straightened, her legs were no longer crossed at the ankles.

Biscuit let out an audible yawn and jumped down to the floor, where he sat for a few seconds before settling into a ball at the base of the ottoman.

"Yes," he said. "Do you know of anyone who hated your husband?"

"You mean more than me because I didn't kill that man, or take Gene."

Paige admired Zach's patience. She was caught up in the rapture of I-can't-believe-this-is-my-life-right-now and was fighting off a case of the giggles. She had to get involved in the conversation or risk losing control of herself.

"What about hate mail, or vicious things that may have happened after the abuse charges?"

Cathy's features relaxed. Her eyes went up and to the right, which indicated she was going to tell the truth. "I remember we received hateful letters after the charges first came up. When he got off, they included death threats. Our house was egged a few times, but as the months passed, so did the harassment."

"Those letters, do you still have them?"

"Oh, heavens, I don't know. Maybe. I can look."

"That would be great."

"So, you really think someone from way back then is coming after him now?"

"Yes, we believe it's possible."

"Oh my." Tension squeezed on her vocal chords and made her voice shaky. "Gene was charged well over twenty years ago."

"We'll need those letters if you can find them."

Cathy stared at them blankly, her eyes misted with tears. "Yeah, of course."

CHAPTER 6

HE KNEW HE WAS GOING TO DIE. The cramping pain that had ratcheted his stomach, faded to the back of his mind. He wasn't sure if the physical ailment was gone or if he had grown accustomed to its presence.

His vision had darkened, and he wasn't sure if it was the deprivation of oxygen, or his body resigning itself to death.

He had hours to think, but the stench of excrement in the water dish kept hitting him in periodic waves. They say the sensory perception of smell shuts off after a couple minutes. It wasn't working for him. He did know one thing for certain though, he didn't deserve to go down like this.

His dead mother had called out to him, appearing as a vision and telling him it was okay to surrender. There was a spiritual realm he would be a part of.

Lies.

When he died, *if* he dared to believe in heaven and hell, he wasn't going where the cherubs plucked on harp cords. He'd be on the fast route to the abyss, with its fiery caverns, and he'd be reporting to the creature with the pitchfork.

Again, if he bought into all that.

Nonetheless, his future was absolute. He would close his eyes, his last breath would exit his body, and in that instant, he hoped he would experience the warmth of forgiveness.

Cathy entered his mind and he wondered where it had gone so wrong. At this moment, he would exchange anything for one more kiss, for the feel of her touch.

He swallowed, his Adam's apple heaving against the constraint of the collar. His legs shook beneath him. He was losing strength.

There was a bench, but it would provide no relief. To reach it would equate to asphyxiation by choker.

Still, despite being nonreligious, he had called out, seeking divine intervention, for someone to hear his cries for help. He met with silence.

The only one listening in was the man who put him here and he had gone silent.

He was guilty of a lot of things, but killing Buick wasn't one of them. If he thought hard enough, he could even remember the dog's soft fur beneath his fingers. He had been a solid fixture, a source of unconditional love.

He would take the knowledge of who ended his best friend's life with him, knowing he hadn't prevented it or had them held accountable.

His captor was right. He deserved to die.

With the absolution, he remembered Sunday school and something the Bible said about the wages of sin being death.

For the first time in his life, he would be debt-free.

He closed his eyes and sank to his knees. The choker tightened around his neck and had his eyes bulging open in panic for air, but any attempts to derive breath were futile.

THE ADVOCATE SAT BACK, his hands clasped behind his head in pride. He had seen another one through and his mission was accomplished, yet again. One less animal-abusing mongrel in the world. One less Offender.

Yes, the earth would be a better planet for the Advocate's sacrifice.

The unfortunate part of his work in the winter was it was impossible to bury the past beneath the surface, and seal it, along with its inevitable truth. But he had other means of keeping the body until the spring thaw. He had placed Simpson on display. He had no such intention with this one.

The Defenseless would not go down without a voice. The crimes against them would have atonement.

Watching the Offender's body hanging there, twitching, was almost too much for him. It tapped at his moral compass, but he silenced it as a weakness. He was the one who carried out justice for those forgotten. He shut the lights off, his thoughts already on the next Offender.

CHAPTER 7

THE ONBOARD SYSTEM RANG, and while it was designed as a safe means of communicating when driving, I still wished that Jack would pull over. The snow continued to fall and I was starting to wonder if it ever stopped.

"Harper and Fisher here."

"Jack, Zach and I just finished speaking with Cathy, Gene Lyons's wife. She remembers getting hate mail, years ago, when all this happened."

"Get your hands on them."

"She's searching now, but we'll have to come back for them."

"Why?"

"She lives in a rat's nest. The entire place is upside down. She asked us to give her a day."

"Another twenty-four hours?"

"I know, Jack, but if we push her, she won't look."

"Fine. You wait for that woman to get her shit together." Jack balanced his hold on the steering wheel with one hand and went searching in his coat pocket for his cigarettes. He tapped one out on a knee, temporarily driving with the tip of an elbow.

My feet flattened to the floor, wishing for a set of pedals so I could at least slow the vehicle down.

"How did you guys make out?" Paige asked.

"Simpson's wife was just as beautiful as it was hinted toward."

I smiled. Jack *was* a man after all.

"But she's a little young, and as it turns out, not the first Missus in Darren's life."

"Did you call Nadia for a full background on her?"

"Why don't you do that and follow up on the one for Craig Bowen."

"The garbage man? Sure."

"Brandon and I are just about to head into a bar."

Paige laughed. "But it's not even noon."

"The kid's thirsty." Jack smiled, the right side rising higher than the left. He put his window down and lit his cigarette.

"Jenna—Simpson's wife," I began.

"You're on a first-name basis with her, Pending? Way to go. Who would have thought of you as a widow hunter?"

"She told us her husband had a new friend in his life. They spent a lot of time shooting pool at a bar named Smitty's."

"We'll catch up on everything later. Get the name and address of Simpson's first wife from Nadia. You go there, and hopefully by the time we're all finished, Nadia will have the information we need on the garbage man."

Jack disconnected the call as the bar's lit sign came into view.

INSIDE SMITTY'S, the smell of paint and wood spoke to its being recently renovated.

Two pool tables were set up side by side near a sign that read *Washrooms*. Dining tables were on the right behind a modest-sized dance floor, with everything else on the left. A long counter ran along the exterior wall as a place for patrons playing pool or dancing to have easy access to their drinks.

The place was empty, except for a man behind the counter who was slicing lemons, or maybe they were limes. I only knew because I detected the aroma of citrus.

He paused chopping. "Sit wherever you'd like."

"We're Special Agents Harper and Fisher of the FBI. We'd like to talk to the manager."

The man set the knife down and wiped his hands on a towel. "FBI? What would you want here?" He threw the towel over a shoulder, snapped his fingers, and pulled out two shot glasses. "Probably something stronger than beer."

"We're on duty," I said.

"Come on, I won't tell your boss."

Jack prickled beside me. "I am the boss."

"Yeah, I figured that but thought, what the hell? So, no drink then?" He shook his head as if we had offended him by refusing his booze, and returned the shot glasses behind the counter.

He pulled the towel off his shoulder and bunched it in his hands. "I'm the manager. Name's Neil Armstrong, and before you make a wisecrack, not the astronaut. What do you want?"

"Do you know this man?" Jack gestured to me and I pulled up a recent picture of Darren Simpson.

Armstrong didn't take the phone from my hand but passed it a cursory glance. "Course I do. The guy's a regular."

"He's dead," I said.

His face showed no emotion.

"He was murdered and left behind in an alley," Jack elaborated, taking the serve back.

"I might have heard something about that."

"Might have?" I asked.

"All right. Something happens to one of mine, I know."

"One of yours?"

"It's no *Cheers*, but we're tight-knit."

"That's great to hear because we think he came here with the man who killed him. Who did he play pool with?"

The bartender laughed. When neither Jack nor I showed amusement, he ran a hand down his face to sober his expression.

"Darren, play pool? He couldn't to save his life."

"Who did he come here with?"

"Let's take a seat over—"

"We're fine standing," Jack interjected.

"Don't let this get out. I'm no snitch and I'm certainly no saint."

My eyes fell to the tattoos that riddled his bare arms.

He leaned across the counter. "The man was cheating on his girl." He slapped both hands on the counter. "There I said it. But don't let it get out because if you do, I'll lose my clientele. What? It's a bar, not a monastery."

"So he never came in here with a man?"

"I never said that. I know the guy friends he'd come in with from time to time. None of them would have killed him."

"How many are we talking?"

The tender curled his lips. "Three, tops."

"We're going to need their names."

"Oh no. I'm not giving out that information. Like I said, I'd be shutting those doors for good if I did. Not going down as a snitch, especially an unemployed and broke one."

"We can get a warrant for your tabs and investigate it that way."

"Do what you have to do. I'm not talking." He faced me. "Am I going to need a lawyer?"

"THE GUY'S AN IDIOT." Jack turned the key in the ignition, but the SUV contested. A second try had the engine starting and cold air blowing from the vents. I rushed to close mine.

"The bar's his livelihood. I'm not surprised he didn't give us much."

"Hmm."

I deduced that guttural response as one not in my favor.

"Call in and get the warrant started for his records."

"Jack, by the time that comes back and we make sense of it, we'll have found the guy."

He pulled out a cigarette and lit up. "I call the shots, Kid, and I want that warrant. I have suspicions myself, and they are telling me a key to our unsub is in those records."

"He could've paid cash, which will leave us nowhere." I wasn't certain why I was being so stubborn and bucking his direction. He gave me a condemning glare that had me wishing I could reverse time a few precious seconds. "I'll get it started."

"Why, thank you ever so much."

Chapter 8

The results on Darren Simpson's first wife were immediate just as Jack had anticipated. Paige had her answer from Nadia in less than two minutes. Her name was Lila Buxton. She reverted to her maiden name when her divorce from Simpson went through.

Buxton's laneway and path were cleared. The snow kept coming down, but the few inches on the pavement testified to it being shoveled not long ago.

As they headed to the front door, a faceless voice called out. "Hello."

Zach had this dazed expression that Paige was sure mirrored her own confusion. At least she wasn't hearing things.

"I said hello." A woman, who was easily three hundred pounds, came around the side of the house. Puffed up further with her winter coat, hat, scarf, and mitts, she was quite round. If her coat had been white, she would have looked like a giant marshmallow. Two dark eyes peered at them through the one-inch opening that wasn't covered by fabric. She pulled down her scarf. "What do you want?"

"We're agents with the FBI." Paige provided the formal introduction. "We're looking for Lila Buxton."

"I wouldn't care if you were merry fuckin' Saint Nick himself. I'm busy." She leaned on the shovel she held, heaving for breath, a cloud of white encircling the air around her head.

"We're here to talk to you about your late ex-husband."

"Ha!" She waved a hand in the air. "The world's a better place without him. I know it might sound cruel to say that, but it's the truth. And before you get carried away, I didn't do it. I thought about it many times, I tell ya." Her tone of voice, which had started off so defensive, transformed into passive.

Paige had a suspicion. "Was he a violent man to live with?"

Her eyes pinched shut as if she were squinting to block out a glare, but Paige saw past it. She was deflecting.

"You must be happy to have him out of your life if that's the case. A guy lays his hands on me once, I'd be outta there."

She studied Paige and then passed the same inquisitive gaze on to Zach. "You talked to his new bitch, haven't you? She sent you this way, swore to the asshole's innocence? Let me guess she fluttered her eyelashes and wore a skimpy little outfit while she did it." Lila's breathing remained labored, but Paige believed it had more to do with the topic of conversation at this point, rather than the earlier physical exertion.

"The reason we're here is because we think you might know who did this to him."

"You mean who killed him. You don't have to pussy-foot around me. Why do you think I'd know his killer?"

"We believe he was targeted because he was accused of animal abuse twenty-six years ago."

Lila laughed, doubling over, the shovel putting in extra duty to hold her up. She stayed in that position for several seconds, holding up a hand and indicating for them to give her a minute.

"Miss Buxton, the person we're after was aware that he poisoned that dog. He was killed in the same manner," Zach said.

She straightened out. "He deserved the way he went out."

"You believe he was guilty? The charges were dropped."

"Only because he knew someone who knew someone. And don't ask me for any names 'cause it would be no good. I don't know them."

"What was it like after he was found innocent of the charges?"

She shook her head. "It was horrible. Partially why we split. The other part, if I haven't mentioned it, he was an ass."

"Did you get hate mail?" Paige asked, thinking back to Cathy Lyons. Maybe if they got their hands on more, they could cross compare.

"Hell yeah. We'd come home from work and the mailbox would be overflowing. Animal activists and such. I remember one clearly."

"And?"

"You'd love to know, wouldn't you? I don't want the bastard to get justice. He deserved what he had coming. Hell, I'd throw a parade in the killer's honor." Lila pointed a gloved finger and drew it between them. "Make sure people care before you ask them for help."

"It's not just about Darren Simpson," Paige started and passed a glance to Zach. "There's another man's life on the line."

Lila laughed. "If he was as much of a saint as Darren was, he deserves whatever's coming."

"Miss Buxton, you have the chance to make a difference."

"I do, already, every day. The whole world is a brighter place with me in it." She sniggered.

Neither of them even smiled.

"I'm sorry that some other animal has suffered at the hands of a madman, but as for this guy killing animal abusers? I say all the power to him. Hell, if he were running for office, he'd have my vote. At least he's doing something about it."

"What do you mean?"

"Just that. Those in power do nothing."

Paige ruminated on the conversation thus far. Lila had mentioned that Darren had beat his charges because he knew someone who knew someone. Was that person someone in higher power? Where they still around? She made a note to investigate the background of Denver's elite.

"You said you received hate mail, do you still have them?"

"From twenty-six years ago? No way. But I do remember where at least one letter came from because I contacted the manager."

"The manager?"

"It came from Humanity Against Animal Abusers. It's an animal activist group."

PAIGE DID UP HER SEATBELT. "Wasn't she a ray of sunshine? We must have expected too much to think she'd have letters like Lyons, but we did get another lead."

Zach flipped on the wipers. They cleared the snow but left a coating of ice.

"Seeing as you never offer to scrape…"

She smiled. "It's not a woman's job."

"You women always want to be seen as equals, so go ahead and take out the garbage, shovel the snow, and warm up cars. Lila Buxton doesn't seem to have a problem with heavy labor."

"I'm not even going there, and you're not as funny as you think you are."

"Then why are you smiling?" Zach hitched his brows and then jumped out of the SUV with the scraper.

As Paige watched him move around in the frigid air, she was thankful for the shelter inside the vehicle. Cool air still blew from the vents, but at least she was starting to get feeling back in her toes.

The onboard system rang.

"Paige Dawson."

"It's time to talk about where we're at so far." It was Jack.

"We'll meet you at the station? Or the local field office?"

"At a restaurant called The Buckhorn Exchange."

Before she could ask for directions, Jack disconnected.

Zachery opened the door, brushed the snow off his jacket, and threw the scraper into the back. "Now where to? I heard the phone."

"To The Buckhorn Exchange."

"What's there?"

Paige smiled. "Dinner."

CHAPTER 9

THE BUCKHORN EXCHANGE WAS DENVER'S original steakhouse. They specialized in menu items not common elsewhere such as buffalo, elk, rattlesnake, and alligator. Taxidermy lined the walls, and, according to our waitress, were hunted by the founders of the restaurant. Management continued to work hard to stake claim to the place being a landmark, not simply a place to eat.

We had already placed our food orders and, of all the meat offered, Paige went with salmon. I wasn't even that adventurous and stuck with beef. I had an eight-ounce tenderloin, and Jack went with a T-bone steak. Zachery ventured and ordered elk. We all declined alcohol and went with coffee or soda.

Jack lifted his mug of coffee. "All right, where are we? Brandon, start us off."

My hand was wrapped around my soda glass, but I didn't lift it for a sip. "We spoke with Simpson's widow and—"

"Was she as hot as McClellan said?" Zachery asked.

Paige's eyes narrowed. "Haven't we beaten that subject to death?"

Zachery defended his position. "How can you talk about a beautiful woman too much?"

"Zach, the case." Jack's voice was all business.

I continued. "As I was going to say, Simpson's widow, Jenna, didn't give the impression of being too consumed with grief, at least at first. When we pushed the matter, her sorrow became more obvious."

"Interesting. Do you think she's hiding something?"

"I'm not sure, but when we visited the bar she directed us to—"

"Smitty's?"

"Yeah. She said her husband had a new friend he hung out with lately and they'd go there to play pool. Only thing is, when we showed up, the manager didn't know anything about a new *male* friend in Simpson's life."

"Oh." Paige's single-word expression held air time.

"Yeah, you're on the right track. It seems the man was cheating on his wife."

"You mean the hot woman?" Zachery warranted a crossway glare from Paige. He shrugged his shoulders and mouthed, *What?*

"What the kid hasn't mentioned yet is, when we asked the manager for names, he sealed up."

"So, what's he holding back?" Paige asked.

"Exactly. Brandon's ordered a warrant to secure the receipts from the bar." Jack sat back in the booth.

The gesture prompted Paige and Zachery to fill us in on what they found.

"Well, you know that Lyons held onto the hate mail and that she's working to dig them up. What you don't know is, Lila Buxton, Darren's wife at the time he was charged, also said that they were recipients of hate mail," Paige said.

"Were you able to get them from her?"

"Unfortunately, no. She threw them out a long time ago, so there's no way that we can compare them to the letters we get from Lyons."

"However, she mentioned that her husband beat the animal abuse charges because 'he knew someone who knew someone.'" Zachery took his napkin off the table and spread it across his lap.

"Hmm."

"Exactly what I thought, Jack." Paige took a sip of her pop. "I want to dig into the history of Denver and see if any names stand out among the politicians."

"Referring to a person as 'someone' could also imply wealth, not just power, but it doesn't hurt to look into it."

"Glad you agree. I called Nadia about it already."

"But that's not all we got from the lovely former Mrs. Simpson,"

Zachery began.

"Zach, you're using the term *lovely* rather loosely." Paige laughed.

It was the deep, throaty one that extended her neck and made her eyes sparkle. It made me smile. She caught my eye and glanced away.

Jack lowered his coffee mug and leveled his gaze on Zachery.

He continued. "She mentioned one letter that she received."

"After all these years? What was special about it?"

"She said she called the company who issued it."

Jack and I both sat up straighter.

"They received hate mail from a company?" I asked.

"Yeah. The company is an animal activist group." Zachery gestured toward Paige. "She searched the Internet on her smartphone on the way here. They're still around."

"You have the name of the person who sent the letter?" I asked.

Paige answered, "No, but we have the name of the manager she spoke to. According to the website, he still runs the place and you're not going to believe who it is."

"I dislike guessing games," Jack said.

"Craig Bowen."

"Bowen? That's the garbage man who found Simpson's body," I said.

"I'm sure they'd prefer the term waste management technician," Zachery chirped in.

"Zach."

"Sorry, Boss. Anyway, the group is made up of volunteers, but Bowen's the leader. Now, while that's interesting, there's more. He's the stepbrother of Kent Fields, the journalist who reported on the animal abuse charges."

I leaned forward on the table and pushed my glass toward the middle. "The man who is a multi-millionaire, winner of Pulitzers?"

"That's him. Bowen would have had access to intimate knowledge of these cases too."

"Possibly hands-on experience with helping the injured animals. Once we get Lyons's mail, we'll have to see if Lyons received a letter from Bowen as well," Jack added.

"I've also been thinking about how far the charges go back. Why go after these people now?" I began. "Does the killer think he'll get away with it? That no one would be paying attention?"

"I agree, Pending."

"Would you stop calling me that?"

Zachery smiled. "Well, it's true."

"I'm a *pending* agent, that isn't my name."

"Cut it out, both of you." Jack shot us a glare. "You're acting like damn children."

I drew my gaze from Zachery. "Our unsub probably figures there will be a lot of suspects to throw us off his track. He might be the least prospective candidate."

"Quite possible, Brandon, or he could be right in front of us." Paige's eyes lit, but she didn't form a smile.

"It makes sense, Boss," Zachery said. "One other thing that strikes me is the bodies of Ball and Garner were never found. Simpson's was. Either the killer has decided to send a message or he wants to be stopped."

"It could be a combination of both," I added.

Our waitress, a petite redhead, came back and set our meals in front of us. "Enjoy. And if there's anything you need, call for me," she said as she'd backed away from the table.

Jack gestured to all of us with his fork. "Like she said, enjoy. Tomorrow's going to be one hell of a day."

Chapter 10

MORNING CAME TOO FAST, which left me hurrying around the room, gathering an outfit from my suitcase—thank God for wrinkle-free fabric—and running out the door. I was determined to do so before Jack came knocking.

I found the three of them standing in the lobby and figured I had gotten there just in time.

"He did decide to join us." Zachery raised his voice loud enough that I was certain the people working the front desk would have heard him.

In fact, a female employee was smiling at me.

"Now that you're here, I'll lay out the day's agenda," Jack said.

I tried to focus on Jack, but my attention kept going to Paige. She was beautiful—kissed by a good night's sleep, her lips a natural pink, her green eyes shaded in a sultry brown, and soft curls framed her face. She loved mornings, and they loved her back.

If there was a way for us to truly be together, without either of us forfeiting our careers, I would give the relationship an honest try. The best we could expect were random and secret rendezvous, and even those, we should probably put an end to.

I dropped into one of the sofa chairs and Jack passed me a corrective glance.

I stood, reluctantly.

"Paige and Zach, I want you to go to the animal shelter where Simpson's dog was brought in twenty-six years ago."

"Makes sense. It's also where Lyons's dog was brought," Paige said.

"Correct. Now, it's the only shelter in the area, but there are a few veterinary clinics. While the injured animals could have been brought to any of these locations, the charges were arranged for through the shelter."

"We'll find out how all of that works, Boss. See if we can find any names that line up."

"Good, and while you're doing that, Brandon and I will be speaking with Craig Bowen."

I was impressed he referred to me by name, and not by Kid or Slingshot. Maybe my standing up to Zachery last night had actually made a difference?

"What about the reporter?" Zachery asked.

"We'll get to him in due time."

"Are you sure he's someone you want to keep putting off?" Paige came back into the conversation. "He has a connection with these cases. He would have seen the people at the time, the animals after they were brought in. He would have seen them fighting for life."

"Once Nadia has his full background, we'll talk to him," Jack replied.

"His stepbrother found the body."

"And that could be completely *unrelated*." Zachery made a play on words and waited for us to acknowledge, but his efforts were lost on Paige, who crossed her arms.

"I'm not dismissing it that easily."

Jack went into his jacket pocket and moved toward the front door, signaling an end to the conversation. The debate was squashed before it gained flame.

Stepping outside, the cold morning air bit my ears and stung my face. It was still dark and the wind howled, kicking up snow from the ground. But, thank God, nothing fresh was falling.

Jack lit his cigarette and hopped into our SUV. I got in the passenger side and watched Paige and Zachery load into theirs.

She had a point, and I wasn't sure why Jack wasn't listening to her. Kent Fields could be working with his stepbrother to exact revenge on these men. The time that had passed would sever the connection and relieve them of suspicion. Maybe that's what the man was counting on. What's that term?—hiding in plain sight.

CRAIG BOWEN WAS OF AVERAGE HEIGHT. He had dark hair, brown eyes, and wore silver-framed glasses. We caught up with him at the city yard when he was getting ready to head out.

His orange snowsuit would be visible in the dark, so it wasn't hard to find him. We walked in his direction, holding up our credentials.

I took the lead. "We'd like to talk to you about—"

"The body I found? It's making me a celebrity around these parts."

"Hey, hey!" Another garbage man called out and pointed at him. "You are the man!"

Bowen dismissed the compliment with a wave of his hand and moved toward his truck. "Now, I'm sure you spoke with my boss to get back here, but I've got a schedule to keep."

"You have ten minutes before you have to head out."

Bowen's face cracked into a smile. "That sly bastard." His arms dropped to his sides and he tucked his hands into the pockets of his snowsuit. "Have at it then." His shoulders hiked upward and didn't return to a relaxed state, giving the saying *shoulders at the height of one's ears* a literal manifestation.

"Had you seen Darren Simpson before that day?" Jack asked.

"No, why would—"

"Think about your answer."

Jack was at it again. The searing eye contact, the locked jawline. His entire aura challenging the man to lie.

"Okay, fine. I saw the man previously, but the whole city did."

"Why?"

"Seriously?" Bowen glanced at me. "You don't know this?" He pointed a finger between us. "You're testing me, aren't you? This is a test."

"We're trying to find out who killed a man, Mr. Bowen." Jack's dry tone propelled Bowen's energy into a regressive landslide.

He held up both hands. "I'll play along. He was in the paper years ago."

Jack and I remained silent.

"For poisoning a dog," Bowen added.

We still didn't say a thing.

"Listen, I don't know what you two—the FBI—want from me, but I didn't kill the guy."

"You found the body."

"Trust me when I say I wish I hadn't."

"Most people would vomit if they stumbled across a body. The only trace recovered from the surrounding area belonged to the victim."

"Sounds like you'll have a tough killer to catch." His eyes skimmed over us to a clock on the wall.

"Surplus of five minutes left. You're still good," I said.

Bowen's eyes shot to me. "I don't know what to say. I can't help you."

Jacked asked what he was doing around the estimated time of Simpson's death.

"What, are you serious?"

"Completely." Jack's face remained indifferent.

"You think I killed the man and staged the find?"

"It would be a good thing to fall back on, and you would have a good reason to want the man dead. You are the leader of Humanity Against Animal Abuse, are you not?"

"Ah, that's what this is about? Yeah, I'm guilty of giving a shit. People abuse animals all the time thinking they can get away with it. You know what the sad part is? They can. They do. All the time."

"Sounds like you have passion."

"I absolutely have a passion when it comes to this. Someone has to stand strong for those animals. God created the earth and put man in charge of caring for them, not in charge of abusing them. Good men strive to make a difference."

"Your records show you're the stepbrother of Kent Fields."

Bowen laughed. "Yeah, good for me, eh? A lot of good it does me. The arrogant son of a bitch hasn't been a part of the family for years. It's almost Christmas and I doubt he's given us a thought. I can't remember the last time we had dinner as a family. He's too big for us now."

I glanced at Jack and worked through my assessment of Bowen. He had motive. He hated animal abusers and made his opinion public. On top of which, he found the body, had a stepbrother who reported on the original cases, and may have had a hand in helping the animals to recovery. If this wasn't enough, his background check made me question his judgment.

"You spent some time behind bars," I said. "Maybe you miss them and want to go back."

"If you had anything against me—proof—we wouldn't be standing around talking." He passed another glance at the clock. "Time's up. Good day, gentlemen. I'd wish you luck in finding your killer, but if he's targeting animal abusers," another shoulder shrug, "I'd say they are getting what they deserve." He reached for the door handle on the truck's cab.

I put my hand on his forearm. "Not so quick."

His eyes went to my hand.

I kept it there a few seconds longer just to prove I was removing it out of my own accord. "You sent hate mail to Simpson when the charges were dropped. We have testimony to that."

Bowen dropped his arm and laughed hard enough that tears seeped from the corners of his eyes.

"Something amusing about that?" Jack asked.

The laughter stopped instantly, as if it were on a soundtrack and someone hit pause.

"Yeah. The fact she, I assume it's the woman Simpson was married to, remembers. That tells me I made a difference."

"She said when she called you, you couldn't have cared less about the death threat you had made on behalf of the organization."

"It was just talk."

"Threatening people's lives isn't *just talk*."

"You must believe me. I didn't kill that man, or no man for that matter. I can't say that I've never thought of taking revenge on these people, but I've never acted on it. The letters, the threats, they were as far as I went."

"So you're confessing to threatening a man's life?" I asked.

"Please don't arrest me." He backed against the truck. "It was a long time ago."

"Any other time I'd take the pleasure, but right now there are bigger things we need to deal with."

Jack gave me a look and I wasn't sure what he was trying to communicate. Maybe I was taking the machismo too far? Oh well, it had to be let out for fresh air sometimes.

"One more thing, if you didn't kill Simpson, maybe your stepbrother did?"

Bowen licked his lips, and his face paled like he was going to be sick. "Hey, anything's possible."

Chapter 11

THE SOUND OF BARKING DOGS resonated through the shelter. The cacophony was comprised of several breeds, the ranges going from a higher octave to a lower register.

The front of the building had a couple of large chained-off areas for animals, but there weren't any out and it likely had to do with all the snowfall they had received yesterday.

Paige had never had a dog in her life, even as a kid, but after she'd moved away from home, her parents had gotten one. They said it would have taken too much to care for kids and an animal, but they now had the time to devote to a pet. Paige didn't buy their reasoning. She put more stock in the house feeling empty after nearly thirty years of having kids in the home. She never voiced her suspicion.

A woman in her mid-twenties approached. She held a cat in her arm and scratched its ears. Its purrs could be heard several feet away. "Can I help you?"

"We'd like to speak to the manager." Paige held up her official ID, as did Zach.

The woman analyzed them. "Well, you've got one of them."

Paige proceeded with the introductions. "And what is your name?"

An extra-deep massage behind the cat's head. "Alisha Clark."

"Do you have some place we can talk?" Paige's eyes fell to the feline in the woman's arms.

Alisha held it up in the air and nuzzled its forehead to hers. "Time to sleep for a bit, my friend." She smiled, a flash of contentment washing over her face, as if the cat could understand everything she said. She placed it in a kennel behind the desk. The cat peered up at her and then headed to the back of the space and curled into a tightly knit ball of fur.

Alisha smiled at Paige. "That's Thor."

Paige laughed.

"Yeah, like in those superhero movies. He's a real fighter and not of this world. Any other cat may have given up, but not my boy. I see it on your faces—I get a little attached, what can I say? I actually helped nurse him back to health and served as his foster care for a while." Alisha paused, assessing them. "I take it you don't know much about what we do here besides let people adopt animals. You do know that much?"

"Actually, part of the reason we're here is to get a better understanding," Zach said.

Alisha leaned on the counter. "You came to ask about what we do here? Something like that could be found on the Internet, I would think."

"We're specifically interested in how things work when it comes to animal abuse cases."

She pulled back, her arms laced tightly together. "What about them?"

"How do charges get filed in a case like that?"

"There's a process. It's not really complicated, but it needs to be followed perfectly, or the bastards walk."

"Bastards?" Paige said.

Alisha's eyes snapped to hers. "Yeah. The dicks who abuse animals."

Paige found the sudden shift in Alisha to be unsettling. "This makes you very angry."

"Damn right it does. There is no reason for it, and the people—if you want to call them that—who do this, they deserve so much more than what they get."

They could have rushed to a conclusion about their unsub being a man. A woman amped on revenge would be capable of most anything as well. Paige had to probe Alisha's statement. "What do they get?"

"Monetary charges, sometimes a little jail time, probation. It's a joke. You know the expression, getting away with murder, well, these people, even when they are—quote/unquote—held accountable, they get a slap on the hand and sent away."

"You think that these people should meet the same fate they inflict on the abused animals?"

Alisha's eyes fired. "I know what the right answer is, but in a just society…When you've seen animals barely clinging to life and realize the only reason is because some bastard used it as a punching bag, or neglected it, it's a test of one's inner character. Before you ask, the fight between right and wrong, that's in all of us. Our conscience, some call it. I can't say I haven't fantasized about exacting the same treatment on these animal abusers."

Paige and Zach remained quiet.

"Something happened, didn't it? I can tell by your faces."

"You don't read the paper, or watch the news?" Zach asked.

She slowly shook her head. "Between here, night class, and another paying job, no. What happened?" She paraphrased her original question. Her eyes clearly communicated she wasn't going to back down until she had her answer.

"A man was murdered, and we believe it has to do with his past. He was charged with poisoning a dog but ended up beating those charges."

Alisha's eyes blanked over. "We haven't had a case like that in a while. We recently brought in a few cats who were given antifreeze to drink."

"This specific instance goes back over twenty years."

"He was killed twenty years ago?"

"No, he was killed last week, but the charges go back that far."

"Oh."

"Oh?" Paige mimicked, hoping Alisha would expound on her line of thought.

Alisha shook her head. "All I know is, I didn't do it. I know what I just said—" She crossed her arms.

"We'd like you to walk us through the process of placing charges,"

Zach said.

"From the beginning? Let's see. We have what we call agents. They are specifically trained in handling these types of situations."

"Types of situations?" Paige asked for clarity.

"When we have to go in and get the animals out of these homes. First, we'll receive a report of abuse. From there we arrange for one of these agents, along with staff from the shelter, to go to the address, and, of course, cops need to be there too."

Paige nodded. "Whenever a formal charge is involved, that would make sense."

"Exactly. That's the gist of it, but basically, just as a lawyer makes a case for the courts, the same is true when it comes to the agent. They are responsible to ensure that we gather everything to support the charge and have this submitted as evidence in the case. If they mess up and forget to log something, it's too late. There's no amendment. A few guilty parties have walked because of this."

"Give us an example."

"Proof of ownership." Alisha adjusted her stance. "First you have to prove that the animal fell under the person's care. Whenever you remove an animal from a property, they must sign off that you're taking them. This serves as proof of ownership. I know in at least one case this let a man get off. He and his live-in girlfriend had over thirty cats. They were tired of them taking over. They called for us to get them off the property. It started off as a plea for help, but when our volunteer told them it would take time to arrange something like this, the man said that if we didn't get there within a half hour, they'd poison the cats."

"What happened?"

"Everything was arranged in a thrown-together rush and we were still too late for some of them. We pulled in and the man was walking back to the house from the barn. He had just laid out the rat poison and antifreeze."

The thought that a human being would do something like this had Paige's stomach churning. "I can't believe people are capable of this."

"You've probably seen a lot worse."

Paige swallowed awkwardly. The woman was right, on a certain level. The victims she sought justice for were humans, but it somehow struck her as worse when the abused were animals. It went against the natural order where men were to care for them. She spoke her thoughts out loud. "I'm used to seeing people taking out their own perverse justice against other people, but not their aggressions on an innocent animal." Realizing that she phrased it *used to* seeing made her realize how callous the job had made her.

"It is rough to witness."

"So what happened in this case?"

"The one with the cats? The property owner signed off for every cat removed, but these weren't submitted as evidence, and once you've had your say, well, you're done there."

"They walked?"

"Yep. And sadly, this happens more than it should. The agent is responsible for ensuring everything is filed properly. That's the point of training them, and they are to have an attention for detail. If they don't, then they are of no use to us."

"What about photographs? Aren't these taken as evidence?"

"Yes, but without the proof being submitted, our hands are tied. Here's another sad fact. We were called out to a farm once. This horse's hooves were so long, they were curling upward. They got a five thousand dollar fine and were put on probation for two years. That meant two years later they could get themselves another horse and abuse it. The cycle would be able to start all over again."

Listening to Alisha tell these stories made Paige empathetic toward their unsub. Typically the driving force to stop a killer was to bring about justice. On this case, the line was blurred. "You mentioned that these agents are integral. So what happens when an agent fails to do their job properly? Do they get let go or can there be charges laid against them?"

"They are reviewed, and if it was negligence, they'll be let go."

"Being an agent is a paid position?" Zach asked.

"Absolutely. While most of us at the shelter are volunteers, there are a few paid positions. Supervisory staff, agents, vets, fund managers."

Paige regained eye contact with Alisha. "Fund managers?"

"The person who manages the shelter, ensures we have enough money to keep running. They are also responsible for arranging fundraisers, but the bulk of our support comes from our volunteers and donations."

Paige had a thought and wanted to see it out. "You mentioned donations? Do you have regular contributors?"

"Of course."

"Could we see that list?"

"With a warrant. I'm sorry, but if I just handed it over I'd lose my post here, and even though I'm not paid, I love my work."

"I can understand that, and if we had questions on a specific case?"

"You'd best be speaking with the manager who runs the place."

Paige nodded. "And their name?"

"Kim Delaney. I can leave a message for her to call you."

"That would be great."

They were on the move when Alisha shouted out. "If you're interested in knowing our bigger donors, you could always check the plaques on the wall on your way out."

Zach was already pointing to one.

Chapter 12

Jack and I were on the way to visit the journalist, Kent Fields, at his downtown condo.

I was happy to see that the weather was holding off. Even though the forecast called for more snow, we hadn't seen it yet.

Fields' building was located in a wealthy district that attracted those who made a minimum seven-figure salary, if not more. Anyone with less money would have shied away, preferring the comfort of an older subdivision, or a new development geared toward lower level income families.

Inside, a man in a light blue suit was positioned behind a front desk. "Good day, gentlemen. What can I do for you?" Based on his self-elevated aura and the purr to his voice, he considered us below him. He must have suspected we weren't there to see an available unit.

Jack and I held up our credentials.

He splayed a hand over his chest. "Are you sure you have the right building? Our residents are upstanding citizens. You might have us confused somehow with the condos three blocks over."

Did he think those with a large bank account could do no wrong? In my experience, often the wealthy got themselves into trouble.

"We're here to see Kent Fields," Jack said.

"And you're sure you have the right building?"

"We're not here to play games. We have an appointment with the man, and this is where we were told to come. Either you lead us in the right direction, or we'll come behind your desk, consult the building's layout and figure it out ourselves. And if you push us to that, we'll take you in for obstruction of justice."

Both of his hands went up. "Now, there'll be no need for that."

No audible response was needed. Jack jutted his chin forward. His gaze was intense enough to cut glass.

The man pointed toward an elevator bank. "He's in the penthouse."

"DETECTIVES." KENT FIELDS' BLOND HAIR was near platinum, and his skin tone was so white it bordered on albino. His blue eyes were sharp lasers.

"We're Special Agents with the FBI." Jack's hand went to his jacket and I didn't sense it was in response to a cigarette craving. I wondered if he contemplated pulling his gun on the man for reducing our rank. Instead, he pulled out a photograph and extended it to Fields.

We were still in the front entry of the penthouse—a bright and open space. From this vantage point, the kitchen and eating area were to the right, and a living room was straight ahead to the far end. To the left was a half bath.

Fields looked at the photograph. "Why don't we go take a seat?" He gestured ahead of us. "But first, please take off your footwear. My maple floors wouldn't take so kindly to the moisture."

We adhered to his request and went into the sitting room. I sank into the most comfortable couch I had ever encountered. I ran my hands along the fabric—soft, like crushed velvet. Jack sat beside me. Fields had taken a detour to the kitchen.

"Can I get either of you something to drink?"

"No, we're fine," Jack called out to him.

I detected irritation in his tone. Fields was taking too long to sit still and seemed to be avoiding the conversation we needed to have with him. Finally, he sashayed into the seating area, holding onto a martini glass, pinching the stem between his fingers. His other hand held the photograph.

He dropped into a chair and crossed his legs away from us. One long draw from his glass before he set it on a side table. "All right, what can I do for you?"

Jack's neck held a steady, tapping pulse that had a cord bulging. He was too aggravated to speak.

I pointed to the picture. "Do you recognize him?"

"Absolutely, but I'm not sure what he has to do with me."

"He was found murdered behind a bakery in town a few days ago."

"Well, *c'est la vie*, right? I mean, we live, we die."

"You don't seem too upset over the loss of life," Jack observed.

Fields centered his line of vision on Jack. "I didn't really know the man. We weren't close. Should I be grieving?" Fields lifted his martini glass for a brief sip.

"How do you know him? You said you recognize him."

"I used to report on local news. See how far I've come." He spread his arms to take in the space, and to guide our eyes to the walls full of commendations and awards. "Three Pulitzers."

"How lovely for you, but that's not why we're here."

Fields' eyes flickered with egotistical insult and he picked at the material of his pants. After a few seconds, he said, "I remember this man, the one who died, was charged with poisoning his dog. It was said to be rat poison."

"You have a very clear memory of something from twenty-six years ago," I said.

"Don't think anything of it. My mind works like that." He pointed to his glass. "This isn't the real deal. A true master of his craft wouldn't dilute his brain matter with the vice of alcohol." He flashed a sly grin. "Here you thought I was drinking mid-day. Stereotypical writer, you probably thought. Well, I'm most certainly not that. I am unique. One of a kind."

I swallowed the urge to edit his inclination toward redundancy.

Jack stood and paced the floor. "Yes, we know. You are award winning. Less of the resume and more on topic."

Fields' brows furrowed downward and his mouth gaped open. His eyes read, *why I never*.

"We spoke with your brother," I began.

"I don't have a blood sibling. You must mean my stepbrother.

Please, he collects trash."

"You write it."

Fields twisted to see Jack. "If you've simply come here, to my home, to insult me, you can both leave."

"Well, isn't it true? Your first years weren't the glory days. You reported on animal abuse cases, local news." Jack dropped into another chair.

Fields watched his every move.

"How did writing this rubbish make you feel?"

Fields' eyes held concentration, and his lips held the curl of a snarl. "Angry. I was so much better than that. And I have proved it. Look around. Local news will not get you a million-dollar condo."

"Multi, from what I understand." I was going with feeding his ego, toying with him, while Jack sought to derive the answers we desperately needed through berating him.

"Tell us about the man in the photo, your viewpoint," Jack said.

"His name was Darren Simpson. Before you think any more of it, I watch the news and I know all the details. Craig even called me when he found the body. He left a message on my voice mail. I never called him back." Fields' gaze fell somewhere behind me.

I shrugged and it served to align his focus. "Family can be like that sometimes. He doesn't think of you as being close either. So no harm."

A glaze skimmed over Fields' aura. He was fine as long as it was his choice to remain aloof, but when that decision was made by someone else, that equated to him being rejected and was a different matter.

"Do you know why he called you?"

Fields shook his head.

"He thinks you might have killed the man." It was a stretch, but I was curious where it would lead.

Fields uncrossed his legs. "This is absurd, the most absurd thing I've ever heard—and I hear a lot."

"You reported on Darren Simpson," Jack said.

"Yes, but I never killed him."

"You also reported on Gene Lyons."

"Lyons? Sounds familiar. Do you have his picture?"

Jack pulled it out and handed it to him.

Fields considered it briefly and gave it back. "Yes. Animal neglect if I remember correctly."

"You really do have an awfully good memory ."

"Don't read anything more into it than that."

"What were you doing—"

Fields shook his head again. "Nope, I'm not going to do it."

Neither Jack nor I said anything.

"You mean like an alibi? Huh." Fields paused. I surmised the quietness of the condo mirrored the emptiness of the man's life. He had the material possessions, but behind the pride, I believed he was alone.

"That night," his eyes went from me to Jack, "I was with someone."

"We'll need her name."

I caught Jack's eye and wondered if he had missed picking up on Fields' apparent sexual preference, or if he were somehow trying to demean the man again. Perhaps Jack hadn't advanced to the twenty-first century yet.

"It wasn't a she. And I'm not going to give you the person's name. That would be a violation of their privacy."

"You're a potential suspect in a murder case, and in the disappearance of Gene Lyons."

"No, I didn't do any of what you're saying. If I give you his name, please do not let this get out to the press."

"You're in the spotlight all the time with those awards of yours, and you don't think people know you're homosexual? Besides, one would think people in your circles would understand and embrace you for who you are," I said. It warranted a glare from Jack. He must have resonated more with the old-school philosophy that stemmed back to Adam and Eve—an irony, as he wasn't a religious person by any means.

Fields' shoulders sagged for a fraction of a second but lifted as a smile lit his face. "You are right. It's time for me to be happy. It's Kent's turn."

The guy was an egomaniac, a textbook narcissist. The referral to himself in third person twisted my gut with suspicion. The persona he presented was that of an individual who had most things together, yet the opposite seemed true.

My mobile beeped with a message. I generally wouldn't check it at a time like this, but I had a hunch it was important. As I slipped my cell out, Jack stared at me, condemnation firing from his eyes.

"His name is Henry. He makes me happy." Kent went on to share his story with Jack.

My attention was on the text from Paige.

I put the phone back in my pocket, and both men watched me.

"You are a generous contributor to the animal shelter in town," I said to Fields.

"Is that a bad thing?"

"It's a suspicious thing."

Fields rubbed his hands on his thighs.

"I'm being set up."

Jack laughed.

A touch of red burned in Fields' cheeks. "What is so funny? This is a joke. My stepbrother put you up to this."

"I assure you it's no joke."

"Where is Gene Lyons?" Jack asked.

"I don't know. I have nothing to do with any of this. You take me downtown and I'll lawyer up."

"Sounds like he's trying to make a deal, Jack."

"We don't make deals with killers. Get up."

I pulled out a pair of cuffs. It had been a while since I'd had to use them.

"Please, just pull my financial background. You'll find that I support all types of local charities. The food bank, the Salvation Army, the Catholic Church. I need write-offs. Please, just tell me this, why do you think I'm guilty? Tell me that and I'll come with you—"

"If we want you to, you're coming with us."

"What do you—"

"The evidence is stacking against you. Your stepbrother found Simpson, a man whom you reported on twenty-six years ago, a man who got away with poisoning a dog, a man who was, in turn, killed by poison."

"That's my point. Twenty-six years ago. Why would I bother at this point?"

"That's the easy part. To allow separation between you and the victim," Jack said.

"Okay, I get that viewpoint. But I didn't do this. I swear to you."

There was something about the shaky nature of his voice, the pleading in his eyes. "You said you are being set up. By whom?"

"I have a lot of people who hate me."

"You'll have to do better than that. Come on. Let's go." I prompted him to stand.

He shrugged out of my reach. "I don't know who would do this, all right, but I know I didn't."

"You're full of helpful information."

"Please, if you had reason to arrest me, you already would have. We wouldn't be sitting here talking."

"We're going to need all the information on your friend Henry, the one you spent the night with," Jack said.

"Fine. I'll get it for you. Please, just know I didn't do this."

CHAPTER 13

THE ADVOCATE HAD SEEN THE news and was extremely proud of his latest accomplishment. He was being acknowledged by the FBI. They were aware of his work. Now, he would have to up the level of skill and choose his next victim—carefully and swiftly. He had no time to give way to self-doubt. He intended to outwork his purpose to its greatest potential.

In an ideal world, the stalking part was the most tantalizing to him. It was a game of cat and mouse, and he was the cat. He would toy with the rodent and paw at it until either he tired of play or it succumbed to his claws.

In reality, he loved playing the position of power and he had truly maneuvered things brilliantly. The murders, the disappearances—they would never be tied back to him. He had done due diligence to ensure that all roads led many places, and away from his front door.

If anything, his lifelong "friend" would take the fall. He'd be the one to receive the full reciprocation of justice, of Karma, of whatever people wanted to ascribe to the righting of wrongs, to the balancing of the universe.

The Advocate had parked down the street, keeping an eye for the most opportune time to make his move. The man he targeted, and longed to spend time with, was another Offender of the Defenseless. He couldn't wait to exact equal revenge. This method would be a first for him.

All good things come in time. The familiar saying rushed in on him, soothing his heartbeat and quieting his thoughts.

It was time to work.

He rang the doorbell.

And waited.

The wind blew alongside the front of the house, penetrating through his plush jacket, to flesh and bone. A shiver shook through him as the door was answered.

This Offender was a giant, but there was one thing not even Goliath could conquer—the accurately placed stone from David's slingshot. Today's modern equivalent was a semi-automatic.

He pulled the gun from his coat pocket, doing so discreetly so that if any prying neighbors were watching, they wouldn't notice.

"Are you alone?" he asked the question, although certain of the answer.

The giant nodded.

"Step back into the house, nice and slow."

"Who are you? If Guy sent you, tell him I'll have his money in two days."

"In the house."

The giant took a few steps toward him, and the cowardice that resided within him registered a second's hesitation. After all, he was the one with a loaded gun.

"All I have to do is scream," the giant said.

"And all I have to do is pull the trigger. Your screams would matter little once your dead body hit the floor." The Advocate's full confidence had returned. His commitment to this mission reinforced.

The man stepped backward into his house, both hands held high.

"You're going to put on your coat and boots and come with me."

"Why would I—"

He shook the gun in front of the giant's face.

He complied and got ready.

"Now, we're going to get into my car, and you're going to act like we're best friends. Got it?"

"Yeah."

This was easy-peasy.

There was only one thing that could make the execution of justice that much better, and that would be clear roads.

CHAPTER 14

THE TEAM WAS GOING TO the local FBI field office to discuss what we had discovered so far, but Paige received a phone call from the animal shelter's funding manager, Kim Delaney. Jack told them to go by and find out what they could from her and meet back up with us later on.

Cathy Lyons had dropped off the hate mail, so we had time to review that while we waited. At least I was working through the pile of letters. Jack had stepped out to grab a coffee from the bullpen.

"How are you making out?" Detective McClellan cast shadows from the doorway into the conference room we were set up in. A visitor's badge dangled from a lanyard that was around his neck.

"People are crazy." I looked back to the letter in my hands, thinking maybe he'd take the hint to leave me to it.

He took a seat. "I heard you guys spoke to Fields."

I wanted to ask how he knew but assumed Jack may have mentioned it.

"You know when we questioned Bowen…dang." McClellan shook his head. "We should have pressured him more. He's the guy's stepbrother."

"Well, don't beat yourself up over it. We haven't proven he's the killer. We didn't even think there was enough to bring him in for questioning at this point."

"I know," he waved a dismissive hand. "It's just this Fields guy wrote the columns on Simpson, Lyons, even the two who were never found from two thousand nine and ten."

"Ball and Garner."

"Yeah. And here the guy's stepbrother found Simpson's body. Kind of coincidental."

"The same stepbrother who runs the animal activist group you directed us to." Maybe staring at the obvious wasn't the answer...

McClellan let out a staggered exhale.

I'm not sure why I had the urge to soothe the man's conscience. "You can't catch everything."

"Yeah, but that's a big one. I still can't buy why Fields would want to throw his life away."

All of this talk about Fields made me want to follow up with Nadia to see how she was making out with his full background and his alibi for the night Simpson was murdered.

"Fields is a large contributor to the shelter," I said.

"Heard that too."

I thought about our conversation with Fields. It was a possibility Jack and I had spent time with the killer. If Fields was behind this, he had a brilliant setup. Pulling from such distant cases, it would put time between him and his victims, but it also proved he had a connection with them. It really wasn't that far of a stretch to contemplate Fields behind the murders.

He had contributed heavily to the shelter, enough to warrant a plaque. He stood up for animals in need of a home but did that mean he went so far as to exact revenge on those who abused them?

My reasoning led me back to Fields' words about charity. He didn't just donate money to one pot, as it were. He spread out his generosities, tax write-offs, as he so kindly put it. There wasn't passion igniting his voice when he spoke about Simpson or Lyons. He remained factual. Was that to serve as a protective front, or was that truly how he felt toward them and, by extension, was it out of apathy?

Jack walked in and nodded toward McClellan.

"It seems like you two have a lot of work ahead of you. Let me know if you could use some help." The detective excused himself.

This case made it hard to distinguish the good guys—was that us or the killer? There was something about a person carrying out vigilante justice in defense of abused animals that held a nobility to it. It played on the heartstrings of mankind's instinctual nature to right wrongs.

"Find anything, Kid?" Jack pressed the mug to his lips.

"Just a bunch of people with extreme hate in their souls. This is a tough one."

"What is?"

The reflection in his eyes revealed he was using this time to analyze and judge my character.

I chose my words carefully. "It's our job to find the killers, to stop them. Usually, it's easy."

Jack squinted for a second as if blocking out sunlight.

I went on. "It's easy in the sense of, it's in our programming. But with this case, we have a killer who is targeting animal abusers."

"You think they got what they had coming?"

"I never said that, but it's one of those moral debates. Do you consider it a success to stop a man who is making the world, in a way, a better place?" It was obvious my words didn't please Jack, based on the reflection in his eyes.

"We have a judicial system in place to determine guilt or innocence. Our unsub is assuming the position of judge, jury, and executioner."

"You know what I mean." I paused for a few seconds and added, "Don't you?"

A slow nod, almost as if he didn't want me to pick up on it.

"You probably don't think I have a heart, Kid. But things in this life are not always fair. It's about acceptance." His eyes darkened and, based on that and the energy in the room, I had a feeling he was going back to his days in the military before he came to the FBI.

Was Jack actually going to open up to me? His next words confirmed my suspicions.

"When you're serving this country, you follow orders. You kill because you are told to kill. The men you shoot have done nothing to you on a personal level. You are fighting for an ideal."

Jack didn't make eye contact with me as he spoke, but I wasn't going to say a thing until he was finished talking. I didn't want to discourage him. This was the most personal conversation we had ever shared. This investigation was even testing Jack's moral servitude.

"It doesn't make you wrong. It doesn't make you right. It makes you compliant."

The emphasis he placed on *compliant* was stamped with disgust.

His eyes found mine. "We stop this guy because that's our job. We don't have the novelty of looking the other way, or even of empathizing with him. This man has murdered at least one, likely more. We don't even know if Lyons is alive at this point."

"I understand, Jack."

His eyes seemed to assess my resolve. Seconds later, he opened his arms to take in the table. "What have we got?"

"The smartass answer—a lot of hate mail."

Was that amusement in Jack's eyes?

"The detailed answer—I've been making a list of names. None of these have had return addresses so far."

"Not a real big surprise."

I reached for the next in the pile and my extremities fell cold. I paused all movement.

"Kid?"

"I spoke too soon." I held up the envelope so he could see.

Jack was on his way out the door, flinging his arms into the sleeves of his coat. I hurried to catch up.

CHAPTER 15

"THANK YOU FOR SEEING US ON SHORT NOTICE." Paige extended her hand to Kim Delaney.

Zach was already seated in one of the two chairs across from Delaney's desk.

"I want to help out however I can. My volunteer told me that someone is killing animal abusers?"

"Seems so, yes. We spoke with Alisha this afternoon and while she was helpful, she couldn't give us all the information we were after." Paige's phone vibrated in her pocket, but she ignored it.

"How long have you been with the shelter?" Zach asked, tracing his fingers along one arm of his chair.

"I've been here fifteen years, but I have records in the computer going back thirty. Even when case files were all handwritten, they were scanned and entered into our database. These days we mostly input our notes electronically. Technology is a wonderful thing. Alisha had mentioned she requested a warrant. I assume you have that with you?"

"Unfortunately, not yet. Those things take a little more time."

"Oh." Delaney clasped her hands in her lap and leaned back into her chair.

"We're still hoping you can help us out."

"I'm not sure if I can, but I'll try."

"Alisha mentioned most of your help comes from volunteers. We'd be interested in hearing about any who volunteered or worked here twenty-six years ago."

Delaney's eyebrows lifted. "Twenty-six years ago?"

Paige pointed to the monitor and threw in a sly smile. "I'm sure you have that in your computer there."

"I do, but I think that would require a warrant too."

"What about any new volunteers or employees?" Paige asked.

She and Zach had discussed this on the way over. While their original feeling was the killer was associated with the shelter twenty-six years ago, it was possible it was someone new who had access to old files. While elements in the case directed them toward Fields and Bowen, at this point, they couldn't provide their names to Delaney.

"We got a new one six months ago. A nice fella. I'm sorry I can't tell you his name without the warrant."

Paige realized how they were pressuring for information while being unable to share any themselves. She needed to disclose the urgency and hoped it would spark the woman to speak. "Another man is currently missing. In fact, there are three total."

"Three?"

Paige had to put her vibrating cell phone out of her mind.

"The help you provide may result in saving a man's life. If we wait on the warrant, it may be too late."

The severity of her suggestion struck Paige after her words came out. They were the FBI, they did everything by the book. They had a high closed case rate and they couldn't risk evidence being dismissed on a technicality.

Delaney angled her head. "I know what you're doing, and I want to help, really I do, but I can't jeopardize my position here. With the economy the way it is, who knows how long it would take to find another job."

"I understand."

Paige and Zach moved to get up.

"Not sure if it will help you, but we had a baseball team this summer. We didn't do half bad." She pointed to a framed print on the wall to their right.

Paige found the detour interesting. Alisha had done something similar when they were here yesterday. She walked over and met up with Zach.

In the photograph, a bunch of smiling faces were staring back at them. There must be someone in the crowd…

Delaney came up behind them. "Recognize anyone?"

Paige did one final scan of the picture and frowned.

"Sorry, I couldn't have been more help."

PAIGE TOOK OUT HER CELL. "What is up with this phone? It's been vibrating nonstop. Three messages."

"So while we were in there on business, you've been having pleasure." Zach laughed.

"Again, with the thinking you're funny." Paige went to press the button to retrieve voice mail when it rang again. "Agent Dawson… okay, slow down…right…we'll be right there."

"What was that—"

"Jack and Brandon are on the way to pick up Craig Bowen, the garbage man. Apparently Lyons's letters were dropped off at the station. He sent them a letter too."

CHAPTER 16

HIS BREATH EXITED THROUGH CLENCHED TEETH. He bucked against the restraints, but he couldn't break free or even loosen their grip on him. He had been fighting against his bonds for what seemed like hours.

He had craned his neck back, and the nausea tightened its hold on him and forced him to empty his stomach contents. His arms were hoisted above his head and the chains were secured to the hitch of a truck.

The reason he was here had become apparent. He had read about the guy who was found dead in an alleyway beside a dumpster. He must be next on the psycho's list.

He should have taken the bullet. There would have been less pain, he surmised, and a higher probability of survival.

"Let me out of here!" he screamed but reaped silence.

The smell of gasoline and oil wedged up his sinuses and the concrete was like iced slate against his back. He was aware of each bone in his spinal column.

"Let me go." His last word lost strength.

Bright lights flickered on overhead, and the truck's engine rumbled as it came to life.

His captor was in the cab.

He squinted his eyes, trying to help them adjust. "Let me—"

The man came around the back of the truck, tapping a crowbar in his palm.

"You make me this person. I am not this person." His captor's mouth curled, twisted, and contorted as if he fended off tears.

Did madmen cry?

"What do you want from me?"

"I want you to die."

Any evidence of conflicting emotion retreated—slipping beneath a radiating murderous intent.

"Why?" His single-worded question echoed back to him. He was aware of the answer.

"You know why, Clyde. You know."

He dropped the crowbar.

Clyde shimmied to avoid having it become one with his leg and escaped its impact by a mere few inches. It hit the concrete, the metal ringing out.

The man laughed. "You will be experiencing so much more pain than that, but nothing more than you deserve."

Clyde envisioned freeing himself and stabbing this man to death with the crowbar. The visualization fed him bravado. "You won't get away with this."

"I do all the time."

The way peace and relief blanketed the man's face sent a tingle up Clyde's back.

"As soon as things get dark, we're going for a little drive. Until then, rest up. It's going to be a long night. Especially for you."

He returned to the cab of the truck. The door didn't close behind him and the engine was turned off.

Now what? He was just being left here to wait?

His captor's boots fell heavy on the concrete as they advanced.

"One more thing—I can't stand crying and pleading, so do me a favor and shut the fuck up." He kicked Clyde in the ribs and blinding pain stole both his vision and his breath.

Blinking back tears, he made out the man coming toward him with a roll of silver duct tape.

"I won't say...a word...promise." Clyde could barely form the plea.

"Now, now. A man like you. Your word means noth—" His captor's head pivoted toward the front of the garage.

Clyde had thought the banging he had heard was his mind

playing tricks on him, but it seemed the man heard it too.

"Seems we have company." He hurried to secure the tape through Clyde's mouth and wound it tightly around his head a few times. Afterward, he walked off whistling.

CHAPTER 17

WE WERE HEADED OUT TO pick up Craig Bowen and were going at it full force.

We met up with Paige and Zachery on a side street and planned an organized attack that would see us both pulling into Bowen's driveway at the same time.

McClellan and Hogan had taken an unmarked sedan past Bowen's house and had confirmed the suspect's vehicle, a black Dodge Ram, wasn't in the driveway. His secondary one, a compact car, was there.

We made our move.

Within seconds, I was pounding on the door. Jack was to my left with his gun readied. Paige and Zach were around the back of the house.

I knocked again.

No sounds came from inside.

"FBI! Open up!" I yelled.

"Looks closed up back here." Paige's voice came over her headpiece to the rest of us.

"We go in. Nice, slow, methodical," Jack directed.

I worked the lock, something that had become a specialty of mine these days. I twisted the handle and, in seconds, I opened the door for Jack.

The seal of the door broke and we stepped inside. I heard Paige and Zachery coming through the back about the same time.

We swept the house in less than a minute.

"He's not here," I said, stating the obvious and making it tempting for Zachery to retort with something smart.

He let the opportunity pass.

I continued. "There's only one other place he might be. We know he's not at work, based on time of day. He might be at the animal activist center."

"Great thinking. Let's get over there," Paige said.

All of us were racing for the front door with no concern over the unlocked house.

"WHAT ARE YOU DOING HERE, Mother?" He hugged her, putting as much love into the embrace as he could muster. If she realized her son was a killer, she'd drop dead of a heart attack. "Why don't you come inside, out of the cold?" He took a couple of steps back.

She smoothed his hair and studied his face. The skin around her eyes creased, the result of aging, but her spirit hadn't advanced much beyond her thirties. She was mature but held a spunky nature that he adored. He only hoped that his life's work would make her proud, but his real calling was one he would never share.

"I'm going to guess you're working?"

He conducted a quick visual examination of the garage. His captive was bound behind a truck and out of sight, the space there only appeared occupied by dark shadows. "Look where you found me, Mom."

"Yes. You spend way too much time in this bloody place. Make your mother some coffee."

He regarded the pickup, thinking more of the man tied behind it, ready to grant him his fifteen minutes of fame, but he'd have to wait.

He smiled at his mother. "I always have time for you." He guided her to the small kitchen, hoping the tape gag held out.

MCCLELLAN'S VOICE CAME over the speakers in the SUV. "Cars are already on site. There is a vehicle in the lot, but it's not Bowen's. Maybe he's parked out back."

"Just keep an eye on the place. We'll be there soon." Jack disconnected, pulled out a cigarette, and lit up. He balanced the wheel with the heel of one palm.

I hated it when Jack didn't have two hands secured on the wheel when he drove. To make things worse, snow had started to fall while we were searching Bowen's house.

"There it is." I pointed to the warehouse-type building that the activist group rented. According to the record, they only occupied a portion of it.

Jack connected with McClellan. "Run the plates on the car."

Two seconds passed and we had our answer.

"It's registered to Felisha Fields. That's Bowen's mother, who married Kent Fields' father."

"Got it."

In less than five minutes, we had Bowen in cuffs and secured in the back of McClellan's squad car.

CHAPTER 18

THE ADVOCATE WAVED WITH A SMILE. His mother was buying his pleasantries as he wished her a good day. He had dismissed her with an excuse of work piling up and the need to attend to it. She wasn't aware of what he did, except for "tinker" in the garage, as she'd put it sometimes.

After he had come into money, she never cared to pry into his affairs and how he occupied himself. No, she just took the generous gift he had given her—a few hundred thousand—change compared to the twenty million he'd netted after tax.

Life was late showing up with its bounteous hand extended to him and it was only by a random stroke of luck he had experienced it.

Now, as he had told his mother, it really was time to get back to his work in progress. Phrasing it that way made it sound more official, punching up the emphasis that what he did mattered. Which it did.

While he was certain the law wouldn't feel the same way about his passion, he didn't need their tainted and distorted perception to touch what was just and right. Those he sentenced to the grave were told why they were chosen. He viewed this as a courtesy to the Offenders when they were deserving of none. Their future was sealed in indelible ink from the point they'd thought they could inflict harm on the Defenseless and get away with it.

The rear lights on his mother's Lexus faded from view down the road. With the observation, it was time to act. It was dark, and the hand of destiny need not tap him on the shoulder. He was ready.

THE GARAGE DOOR LIFTED AND Clyde's eyes bulged open. He tried to yell, but it came out as a garbled mess behind the silver tape his captor had secured in place.

Footsteps came closer, and the overhead lights flickered on, causing his eyes to pinch shut in an instant reaction. He reopened them, hesitant, wondering if he wanted to face his death.

Pain from his shoulders slithered up his neck and shot down his spine.

The man looked down at him. "It's time to go for a little ride." He cocked a single eyebrow, and the other barely twitched with the action.

"Why?" The single word was clear in his mind but became jumbled when it exited his mouth.

"Now, now. You know what you did to poor Benjamin."

This *was* about the dog!

The thought occurred to deny the allegations that had been levied against him, but the truth would show in his eyes. Despite all his misgivings, the one thing he was incapable of was lying—ironic enough, seeing as it paled in significance to his other offenses.

"Nothing to say?" His captor smiled. "I guess we're done here." He took a few steps. "I must say it's kind of disappointing, though. I'm used to speeches about innocence and why I shouldn't kill people. Oh well." He accompanied his words with a shoulder shrug and walked away.

"Stop. Plea—" He, again, sounded like a man whose mouth was numbed by a dentist's needle.

The man's steps became faint, only to be superseded by the roar of the truck's engine.

Then it started to move.

CHAPTER 19

JACK TOLD ME IT WAS my turn to handle this interrogation. That suited me just fine.

I spun the chair around, straddled it backward, and tossed a photograph of the letter from Lyons's collection across the table.

Bowen lifted it up, skimmed it, and set it down.

I had yet to question a suspect who came across so calm. He didn't appear to be sweating, or cold—either extreme was evidence that the body was experiencing stress. He returned eye contact and didn't shy away from it.

"What about it?"

"This letter was sent to Gene Lyons."

"I see that." He pointed to the address on the envelope and the salutation at the top of the letter.

"You sent it."

"That is my name right there. I don't understand why you had to raid the place and bring me in, right in front of my mother."

"Where did you take Lyons?" I ignored his protest about the timing of his arrest and tossed another photograph across the table, this one of Lyons on his wedding day.

"A little dated, isn't it?"

"So we've established you sent a letter threatening his life and you know what he looks like."

Bowen rolled his eyes. "Put me in prison already."

His easygoing nature in this situation had me attempting to ascertain whether or not we may have jumped to conclusions about him, despite his tainted background and connection to the victims. I shook any hesitancy about his culpability aside. This man had the perfect setup.

"We spoke to your brother."

"*Step*brother. Don't forget that part."

"He thinks that you're setting him up to take the fall. That you're not man enough to own up to what you've done." I was playing it up to see if I could elicit a reaction.

"The man's a bastard. He's not loved."

"The world seems to love him enough. He's had a very successful career. Your resume isn't quite as impressive. First jail, now you work as a garbage man."

"Waste management technician."

I smirked at the man's ego, recalling Zachery's correction from the other day. Bowen nailed it word for word. It was time to bring the man down a notch. "You did time for stealing investment money from seniors."

"As I told everyone back then, I was the victim there. I knew nothing about what was going on. The owner of the firm was the crooked one. Set up a front, collected their money, and took off."

"The problem with that is you were the one collecting the money and handling the deposits."

Bowen took a deep breath. "That's in the past. I know my innocence."

I stood and paced the perimeter of the room. "What about now, Mr. Bowen? Do you know your innocence?"

He watched my every move.

"You come to the defense of those poor and abused animals. Many people would applaud you for getting even." I bent to reach his ear. "You'd probably even make your mother proud."

"I didn't kill that man."

I slammed a photograph on the table in front of him. "Darren Simpson was his name. He left behind a wife who loved him. You stole him from his family."

"I didn't."

"What about Karl Ball? What did you do with him?" I put his photo on top of Simpson's. "He went missing in two thousand

and ten. He left behind a wife. And this guy." I layered Dean Garner's face on top of Ball's. "He left behind a wife too." I walked a few steps. "Now, I know you're not a husband. Either you never married because you didn't find the right girl or you're just not suitable for that lifestyle. Maybe all of the girls you asked said no. I don't really care."

Again, I was striving to obtain a reaction, but received none. Despite the fact Bowen took pride in his work, he wasn't narcissistic, and that aspect didn't fit with the killer we hunted. Our unsub had his own agenda in which he justified his actions. The reasoning would require someone to think highly of themselves, viewing themselves as above the law. I was starting to wonder if we had the right man, but for now I would do my job and continue on as if I didn't experience any nagging doubts.

"Darren Simpson," I blurted out.

Seconds passed. I said nothing more.

"What about him?" Bowen asked.

I sat back down. "We spoke to his first wife. You remember her?" We had mentioned her at the city yard, but I thought I'd approach things from another angle.

"How the hell do you forget someone like that?"

I hadn't met her, but the breakdown from Paige and Zachery was sufficient to provide a clear picture. I continued. "She said that she had quite the fight with you over a letter you sent on behalf of the activist group you run."

"I thought we went through this, and that was a long time ago."

I leaned on my elbow and lowered my eyes hoping to give the impression I was utterly bored of the subject. "You can't have it both ways. You remember her, but it was a long time ago?"

"Fine. Yes, there was a letter. Yes, we got into a heated argument, but I never killed anybody. If I were going to, I would have done it long before now. Don't you think?"

"Actually, we're thinking it's rather genius to target those with charges dating so far back. It muddles the trail."

"Muddles the trail?" Bowen laughed. "I live in the heat of the moment. I was ready to strangle her, but you know what? My conscience kicked in and told me it wasn't the right thing to do."

"But it's okay to threaten people's lives."

"There's quite a difference between making a threat and acting on it."

I collected the photos and stood. "In the eyes of the law, both are considered crimes."

THE REST OF THE TEAM and Detective McClellan were in the observation room. Only Paige paid me any attention when I entered.

McClellan kept his nose pressed against the glass as he spoke. "He was right in front of us."

I stood beside him and joined his surveillance of Bowen. "There's still a lot more to prove."

"You don't think he did it."

"It's too soon to tell."

"Brandon?" Paige said.

"You heard everything I did. You saw him. He doesn't project guilt. We haven't found any evidence of the victims having been at his home, or at the animal activist headquarters."

"He has a history of threatening people's lives."

"Unless we can pin this murder and the disappearances on him, I'm not sure what else we can do."

Disappointment washed over the team's faces, except for Jack who remained expressionless. His attention was on me, but I couldn't tell what he was thinking.

"The unsub we're seeking would have a narcissistic ego," I began, knowing I didn't need to elaborate on my earlier internal reasoning.

"Bowen doesn't really demonstrate that," Zachery said.

I shook my head. "Besides taking pride in his job, which I consider healthy, I don't think so either."

McClellan leaned against the wall with crossed arms. "If you weren't so sure of his guilt, why did we go in so hot and heavy?"

"Between the hate mail, and his past and current position with the activist group, he was a likely suspect," Paige said.

"Too much so." The words slipped out and everyone looked at

me.

Zachery gestured to the room. "I think our killer is hiding in plain sight."

Something about his words hit me. The ideal suspects were shelter volunteers, the journalist, members of the activist group. Our killer might not fall into any of those categories.

McClellan's phone rang and seconds later, his face pale, he told us what his caller had relayed. "There's been another incident. The guy's still alive—if we hurry."

CHAPTER 20

WE PILED INTO ONE SUV and followed McClellan out to the scene. No sign of an ambulance, so they had likely been and gone. Cruiser lights were flashing. Investigators were combing the road and leaving yellow, numbered evidence markers in their wake. The snow was stained red down the center of the driving lane and it didn't take a genius to figure out how that had happened.

Jack pulled up beside a cruiser where Hogan was leaning on an open door, watching everyone as if he were in charge. He bobbed his head toward us.

"The victim's name is Clyde Ellis. So far, he's still hanging on, but barely."

"I assume you have reason to believe the victim's fate is somehow connected with our case," Jack said.

"The victim is Clyde Ellis and he was charged with dragging his dog behind his truck."

Paige's hand shot up to cover her mouth. "I'm going to be sick."

"Let me guess the charges against him were dropped too?" I asked.

Hogan nodded.

"How could he beat that? You'd think that one would be easy to prove," I said.

The detective looked at me. "Yeah, if you were there watching the act."

"And let me go further out on a limb here. Ellis was charged twenty-six years ago?"

"You got it."

"The killer probably knows we're here," Zachery explained, "to act again so soon."

"He's trying to have the last say. He doesn't think he'll get caught," I said.

"Was there any evidence pulled from the scene?" Jack asked Hogan.

"Crime scene is still processing, but we believe he was gagged with silver duct tape. We found a small piece near his mouth. We think the perp ripped off most of it and took it with him."

"Ellis would have suffered in silence. I can't even imagine the hell he went through. He would have felt his bones break and realized he was going to die—painfully." Paige shook her head, and I'd swear, even in the limited light, her eyes were misted.

The rest of us remained silent for a bit, assimilating what we'd just been told. While some people might argue that violence against others was as natural as breathing and that it went back to the beginning of time there was nothing natural about it.

Hogan picked up again. "We know for certain that Ellis was bound by chains to the back of a truck."

"A truck specifically?" Paige asked.

"Yeah. Based on trace evidence and the damage done to our victim. Broken legs, ribs, back. You get the idea."

Zachery winced.

"My thoughts exactly," McClellan added, speaking for the first time since we arrived.

"Is there any evidence he was given anything to suppress the pain?" Paige rubbed her arms and bounced, no doubt to warm herself.

"Not that we're aware of. We only got a couple words out of him at the scene. He," Hogan swallowed roughly, showing his first signs of empathy, "he said, 'I'm sorry.'"

The impact of the man's last words silenced all of us. Our killer's mission had been accomplished. His victims knew why they'd been targeted and this one was moved to remorse.

"What is the distance from Ellis's house to where he was found?" Jack asked.

"Only three miles."

"Our unsub lives in the area," I offered.

"And he obviously has transportation," Zachery said.

"How far was Ellis dragged?" Paige asked Hogan.

"Investigators have worked their way up the road with a keen eye for any trace of blood and tissue. One thing about the snow, it made things a little easier to spot. The first sign of blood appears one mile from where he was found."

"He was dragged for a mile? I'm going to be sick." Paige's one hand shot to her mouth, and the other to her stomach.

"Where did the trace start? That could give us the location of our unsub," Zachery reasoned.

"It started in the parking lot of a rundown garage. It hasn't been open to the public for years now."

"Do they have a locked gate on the lot?" Zachery wasn't deterred.

"No. Just a sign that reads no trespassing. As if that's going to stop a killer."

Jack pulled on his cigarette, the amber butt glowed in the night despite the strobes of emergency vehicles around us.

"So it could be anyone." The realization dampened any excitement that had started with the thought we were getting closer to our killer. "Who owns the garage?"

Hogan shook his head. "They go south in the winter. Besides there's no trace leading into the building. We believe it's more likely Ellis was bound to the truck in the lot."

Hogan gave it a few seconds and continued. "Now, there were no witnesses who saw him being dragged, but the girl who found him was pretty shaken up. I say girl, but she is in her twenties. She was taking her dog for a walk, to clear her head, when she found him. Said all she heard was moaning at first. Thought it was the ghost of her grandmother."

McClellan rolled his eyes. I took it to mean he didn't believe in an afterlife either.

Hogan went on as if he hadn't noticed. "Anyway, when she realized it was a dying man, she said she screamed louder than a banshee and it took her a long time to calm down enough to dial nine-one-one. She said it took five tries."

I gave voice to what I figured everyone else must have been thinking. "So, she's not afraid thinking that a spirit might be talking to her, but a dying man—"

Jack's glare silenced me. "What's her name?"

"Connie Shepard."

"She's the one who swears to him saying, 'I'm sorry.' She says she asked him what he was sorry for, but he passed out on her."

"Is she here? We'll need to speak with her," Jack said.

"She was pretty shaken up and I had officers take her home." Hogan held up a hand. "We did take her full statement."

Jack's scowl was epic. I wasn't sure if the white cloud around him was the result of smoking, breathing, or actual steam coming out of his ears. He addressed his team. "We will have to speak to Shepard."

"I just told you everything," Hogan protested.

"That was everything?" The derision in Jack's voice licked every word. "It's likely you're missing something."

Loathing flickered in Hogan's eyes. McClellan seemed to be sitting this one out. I can't say that I blamed him.

"We also ran a quick background and a credit check on Ellis. Just the basic stuff but it was enough to confirm he was in debt up to the eyeballs."

"Would anyone benefit from his death?" Jack asked.

"You're thinking a Will? It's too soon to know."

"And the wife?"

"He's single."

"Hmm."

Zachery said, "I don't think this changes anything. The others he targeted were married, but that isn't the basis of his criteria. He's after people who abused animals and got away with it."

"Specifically men who abused dogs," I added.

"Things we've already covered." Jack's jaw was taut. "Back to forensics. Anything else?"

"They found a scrape of chrome paint at the scene," Hogan answered. "They figure it came off—"

"The hitch."

Hogan's eyes snapped to Jack's, but he didn't express his irritation over being interrupted. He left that to his body language.

"Good news is they may be able to match that paint to a vehicle make," McClellan pitched in.

"Yes, they probably can."

Jack's agreement with McClellan had the detective smiling.

I used the opening as an opportunity to voice my suspicion. "Bowen has a Dodge Ram."

"You're forgetting one thing, Pending."

I glared at Zachery. It was one thing to insist on nicknames when it was just the four of us and quite another that he'd pull it out in front of other people. "And what's that?"

"Bowen was in the room with you when Ellis was being dragged along the road like a sack of potatoes."

Paige scowled at Zachery's indelicate turn of phrase.

"What's to say that he didn't do the deed before we picked him up?" I was struggling to regain ground. I hadn't thought everything through prior to opening my mouth. In a lot of ways, I just wanted this case over.

"A quick solution would be to check the hitch on his truck," Zachery offered.

We had found his vehicle behind the activist headquarters.

McClellan waved his finger toward him. "I'll get a uniform over there right away."

I nodded, and, as Paige latched eyes with me, the truth reflected back. I was eager to get home, not for Christmas but for closure when it came to my marriage. I was ready to move on to the next chapter in my life. A part of me envisioned sipping wine with Paige while holiday music played in the background.

I had to focus on business. "What about tread marks?"

"We were able to lift some. Another reason we know we're looking at a large pickup. We're also narrowing down the brand of tire." Hogan passed Jack a glance as if to ask, *satisfied?*

"I assume you're searching Ellis's house for any clues," Jack said.

Hogan let out a breath. "We are. Patrol is watching his place tonight and investigators will get over there by morning."

"Morning?"

"As you can see," Hogan gestured around, "they are pretty tied up just getting the evidence from the crime scene."

"Hmm."

"What do you want me to say? Do you want me to lie to you?"

I took a couple steps back. Apparently the detective didn't take too kindly to being on the receiving end of Jack's infamous 'hmm.' I hoped their egos wouldn't escalate to blows.

Jack disregarded the man. "Paige and Zachery, you'll speak with Connie Shepard. See if you can pull anything else out of her. Find out if there's more she heard him say." Jack pointed to Detective Hogan as if daring him to speak. His cheeks flushed and I imagined the slew of expletives running through his mind.

"Of course." Paige passed Hogan a brief glance. "And you and Brandon?"

"We're going to wait on word back about Bowen's hitch. Take it from there."

Paige studied his face and I guessed what she was thinking. Very rarely did Jack not know everyone's next step.

"So if this latest victim wasn't Gene Lyons, where is—"

My question was interrupted by Hogan's cell. He put his back to us and answered. Not long later, he turned around. "Ellis didn't make it."

CHAPTER 21

JACK'S UNCERTAINTY OVER OUR NEXT step was a brief interlude. The results were in and Bowen was cleared of Ellis's torture and murder. The hitch on his Dodge Ram was in pristine condition and the tire treads weren't a match. He had also come up with a sufficient alibi for Simpson's time of death. He was a free man.

It was ten o'clock at night, but we were headed to Ellis's neighborhood. My argument about people not being helpful at this time of night fell on deaf ears. Jack had his mind set and his temperament fell somewhere between frustration and raw anger. I wasn't sure exactly why his mood had taken a fowl turn. I surmised it could have stemmed from any number of things—Hogan, the fact we pursued the wrong guy, or maybe it was a simpler matter, the nicotine in his system was running low.

We started with the house to the right of Ellis's. At least there was light casting from the front window. It dulled and brightened telling me someone was watching TV.

"I'll handle it if you want," I said, offering out of compassion for the people behind the door.

"That's fine."

I wasn't sure what he meant by that—that I was good to handle this, or that it was all right for me to sit this one out. I should have known better than to pack two inquiries into one statement.

I knocked instead of ringing the doorbell. At least that way if part of the household were asleep, I wouldn't be waking them.

Jack didn't miss my choice and shook his head.

Feet padded along the floor inside, sending vibrations to

the front step. The outside light came on and the curtain in the window was swept aside. A woman's face peered out at us and her eyes enlarged, likely the result of seeing two men on her doorstep at this hour.

I was quick to hold up my credentials. "FBI."

Fear, confusion, and a flavor of distrust tempered the reflection in her eyes, but the deadbolt *clunked* and the door slowly opened.

"We'd like to ask a few questions about your neighbor who lived in number eight sixteen," I said.

The woman let her eyes fall over both of us and came back to settle her gaze on me. She hugged herself. "Why would you have questions about Clyde?"

Her response was promising. She was close enough to her neighbor to know his name.

"Come in. It's freezing out there." Her arms waved emphatically, hurrying us to get a move on.

She closed the door heavily behind us. Either there was no one else in the house to wake up or she didn't care if they did.

She rubbed at her arms. "What do you want to know about him?"

Deciding what to disclose and what to withhold was the tricky part. Ellis's older brother was the next of kin and lived about an hour away. The notification was being worked out by Hogan and McClellan. We had to be careful what we said until that aspect was handled.

"There's been an accident," I said.

"And they sent the FBI? I don't understand. Is he dead? Is his family being told?"

"Yes, of course. We're here to ask you when you last saw Mr. Ellis."

"Why? I don't know." She weaved her arms, her eyes burning with intensity.

"Last week, last night, yesterday?"

"Well, he works at the hospital, in engineering. He wasn't home most days. He must hold odd shifts because I know he'd be home during the week at times."

"Linda, what in the—" A man came into the entryway wearing a tattered blue housecoat and rubbing the back of his head, his hair a matted mess. His robe was open at the front revealing gray boxers. His eyes were blue and set back in a bed of wrinkles from a hard life. There was something about him that didn't place him much over seventy, but he could pass for eighty at a quick glance.

"Be quiet, Lester. This is the FBI. And for God's sake, do that thing up." She waved her hand in front of him.

His brow knitted up like he had the onset of a headache, and he made no move to follow his wife's advice until Jack extended his hand.

"Supervisory Special Agent Harper."

"Whoa, they sent the big guns to our door, Lin."

His wife's arms were no longer crossed but on her hips. She rolled her eyes at him. "They are here about Clyde. Something's happened to him. I think he's dead, but they haven't confirmed that."

The way she expressed herself implied an emotional connection, but whether it be shock or simply the human tug that one experiences when an individual passes, I wasn't sure. No tears sparkled in her eyes and her voice held steady, uncut by emotion.

Lester angled his head and shoved both hands into his robe's pockets. He went and stood by his wife. "What happened? Was he murdered? I mean he must have been for you to be here. Something awful too, I'm wagering."

I glanced at Jack, uncertain if he wanted to pick things up from here or let me continue. I gave it a few seconds and Jack answered the man.

"He was found in a ditch outside of the city. He has since died, but we believe his death was suspicious."

"So he didn't die next door? Oh, thank God." Linda turned heavenward, steepling her hands as if about to pray.

"You'll have to disregard my wife—"

She shot him a glare that could have been a superhero's secret power.

It didn't stop Lester from continuing. "Her one fear is that we'll be broken into and murdered in our sleep."

"I've had that dream since I was eleven." Linda's eyes watered now.

"We believe he was targeted." Jack's words came without feeling, not that it was a surprise.

"Targeted? Why? Who would want to kill Clyde?"

"Do you remember when you last saw him?" I asked. When the couple both seemed to retreat, I added, "I'm sure you can appreciate we can't get into all the details."

They both nodded.

"The last time you saw him?"

"I don't know. I wish I could help." Linda's chin pulled up as if fending off a bout of crying, the news finally sinking in.

"You know," Lester wagged an index finger, "I saw him yesterday, come to think of it."

Linda's eyes grew large. "Lester?"

I glanced at Jack and proceeded. "Where and when?"

"Next door, of course. I don't know. It was about two or so."

The way his wife watched him gave me the impression she questioned his statement.

Lester finally buckled under his wife's stare. His shoulders drooped, his jaw tightened, and he returned eye contact. "What, Linda? I know what I saw."

Maybe it was due to the long day and its events, but I found their interaction amusing. Was this what it was like to be married for fifty years—the judgment, the finishing of each other's sentences, the loss of one's identity? Maybe my divorce was a blessing.

"What were you doing outside at that time of day?" Linda's hands formed into fists on her hips.

"What? Am I not allowed outside without your permission?"

"The doctor said that you're not supposed to be shoveling. We hire that boy down the street to come do it. Are you wanting to leave me all alone?"

I glanced at Jack. His jawline was angled sharply. His mouth sat in a flat line. His patience, which had been almost non-existent when we arrived, was now a quality that couldn't even be pulled out of him.

"Linda. Lester."

Their bickering continued.

"Hello? Please."

The couple fell quiet, and their eyes went to me.

"I'm assuming Clyde was outside when you saw him?"

"Yes, of course." Lester glared at his wife.

She knotted her arms again.

"What was he doing?"

"He was headed out with someone."

Jack's jaw softened, ever so slightly. My stomach fluttered. Had this man seen our killer?

"He was with someone?"

"Yeah. That's what I said."

"Did you get a look at them?"

He was quiet for a few seconds and shook his head. "Not really. I mean, I saw that there was a person in the driver's seat. It wasn't Clyde. I couldn't make out the face. The sun was reflecting on the windshield in just the right spot."

"But you knew Clyde was with them?"

"Yes, definitely. He's a big guy. He appeared hunched over."

"So it was a small car that he was in?"

"Yeah."

"Do you know what make and model it was? The color?" My heartbeat quickened.

"It was a Nissan sedan." His forehead screwed up in concentration. "I don't know the model, but it was red."

"An older vehicle? A newer one?"

"Newer."

"And you definitely don't recall the model?"

"No. Sorry."

"No, you've done very well. Have you ever seen that car there before?"

Lester glanced at his wife and both shook their heads.

"Did it seem like Clyde got into the car willingly?" I took the shot that Lester had seen him walking toward the car, not just in it.

"I did notice he was looking around and walking slower than he normally does. The guy is over six feet and he usually huffs it anywhere he goes."

"And you never saw the driver outside of the car?"

"That's right. I must have just missed him though because I did hear the car's door slam. That's actually what first got my attention."

"All right. You've done an excellent job, Lester. Thank you for your help. And, Linda, thank you." I smiled at her and she returned it.

CHAPTER 22

PAIGE ANY ZACK PULLED INTO the driveway belonging to Connie Shepard, the woman who found Ellis in the ditch. There were three other vehicles there, indicating Shepard had company to support her. Finding a man barely clinging to life would be traumatic.

Lights appeared to be on in every room of the house. There would be no risk of waking anyone up. The house itself was glowing with the colored festivity of the season. A lit, inflatable family of snowmen was on the front lawn. As a grouping, they would have been large enough for a person on a plane to hone in on.

Some people were so tacky when it came to their holiday decorations, but even colored lights were not Paige's thing. She preferred the soft and elegant touch that white lights offered. She also had a thing for the dangling icicle variety if put up in good taste and not overdone.

Her Christmas tree was always accented with white string lights and colored ornaments. She loved her brass pieces, some with glass jewels that sparkled. She didn't have the assortment her mother did, which ranged back through generations of the Dawson family, but she did have her *Baby's First Christmas* ornament. It was a red ceramic stocking with a bear peeking out the top of it. Her name was on the stocking's trim. Her mother told her this piece was hers while the others they had acquired over the years, personalized or not, were to remain in the family home. Paige had made the compromise.

This year, she had only gotten as far as pulling out the box of decorations before she'd headed off to Colorado. Each year she would pick out real trees with her mother—one that would belong to the family home and one that would go in her apartment.

She wondered if they'd get this case solved in time to hunt for trees or even celebrate at home. Her heart was laden by the negative thoughts that took precedence. They *had to* get back in time.

"You coming?" Zach was out of the SUV and butted his head in through the open door.

"Yeah, of course." She smiled, certain it would appear wistful—the way she was feeling.

She understood why Jack had them on this right away, but still wondered if they would have been further ahead to come in the morning. A night's sleep had the tendency to dredge things from the unconscious and provide clarity.

Paige rang the doorbell. It played a rendition of "Silent Night" infusing even more homesickness and nostalgia through her. She expected Connie Shepard's dog to start barking, but nothing. It must have been asleep somewhere or unable to come near the door.

The chime hadn't finished by the time the door was opened.

A woman in her mid-twenties stood there, a rocks glass in her hand, half full of amber liquid. By the way she wavered, it was obvious it wasn't her first drink of the night.

"FBI. We're looking to speak with Connie Shepard," Zach said.

She flashed a goofy grin and pointed a finger back at herself and pressed its tip into her chest. "This is." She took a noisy slurp of alcohol and flashed another smile at Zachery. "And who are you? You're kind of cute."

Maybe it was best that they return in the morning. What were they going to get out of a drunk woman? And if they did get something out of her, how reliable would it be?

"Who is it, Connie?" A man came up and draped his arm around her, letting it dangle over her right shoulder.

"They are the FBI." She kissed him on the cheek—a wet one by the sound of it.

He didn't seem to mind. He pulled her in tighter, smiled at her briefly, but leveled a serious gaze on them. "She's been through an awful lot today. Questioned by the cops about what she found. I think you should leave her alone." His eyes were glassy. He had been drinking along with her.

Paige could see, behind the couple, there were a few others who were also drinking. One guy scowled at her. That confirmed it.

"Perhaps, we'll come back in the morning."

"Good idea." Connie's boyfriend slammed the door.

As they walked down the steps, loud music poured out of the house.

Paige jacked a thumb over her shoulder. "Guess she found the medication to help her cope with what she's been through."

"It's not her I'm worried about right now."

"Jack?"

"Yeah, how's he going to react when we tell him we didn't speak to her tonight?"

She patted Zach's shoulder and laughed. "Well, technically we did. We just didn't get anywhere with her."

CHAPTER 23

THE NEXT MORNING, we were in the hotel's restaurant taking advantage of the continental breakfast. The spread of empty carbs was astonishing. There was a hot tray of scrambled eggs and one of pork breakfast sausage—I said no thanks to the latter.

My plate had appeared like I was on some sort of egg diet before I had scarfed it down like a man who wasn't sure when his next meal would come. With it, I drank enough coffee to fuel a transport truck. Paige and Zachery picked at their food while Jack was finished and had an unlit cigarette perched between his lips.

"There wasn't any sense in pushing a drunk woman to talk," Paige said. Defensiveness was written on all her features, and her cheeks held a touch of pink. Somehow when she was charged up for a fight, she was even more attractive.

Jack removed the cigarette from his mouth and tapped one end on the table as if it were a pen. "I asked you to speak with her."

"I understand that, and we tried." She broke off a piece of her croissant and popped it into her mouth. It had me wanting to kiss the butter from her lips.

Her mouth formed a brief pout after she swallowed her food. "Jack, she wasn't in any condition to talk to us. Trust us on that."

Jack stopped tapping the cigarette.

No one else seemed to get away with speaking so directly to Jack. I wondered if it was because she was a woman or because she was Paige.

She filled in the silence. "We'll go over there right after breakfast. It's possible something shook loose overnight."

"Hmm."

"Jack, you understand. I know you do."

His eyes slid from hers to mine, as if I were involved in what he viewed as a conspiracy.

"At least the kid and I made headway last night," Jack said.

Paige put another piece of croissant in her mouth.

"Turns out the neighbor saw Clyde Ellis leave with another man."

Zachery thrummed his fingers on his coffee mug. "So we have an ID?"

"Not even close, but we have a red Nissan."

"A newer model," I added.

"Did Ellis seem to know the person he left with?"

"According to the neighbor, Ellis was following behind. It rules out that the man was holding a gun on him." Jack slipped the cigarette back into his mouth.

"Okay, well, he could have been coerced in another way," Paige said. "It still doesn't rule out the use of a gun. The unsub could have been cautious that maybe a neighbor was watching. The underlying threat of being shot still a viable one."

Zachery got up and went to the coffee carafe, which wasn't far from our table.

"Makes sense," I said.

There was something at the tip of my brain, but I couldn't quite pull it out. It fell just out of grasp, but once I got a hold of it, it would probably prove to be a revelation that would steer the case.

Zachery returned with a refreshed cup of coffee. "Ellis could have known his attacker and trusted him."

"Good thought, Zach." Jack offered the compliment, and I strained my neck to face him. He rarely offered praise.

I flashed a smirk at Zachery, the expression probably coming across as if I had been poked with an electrical prod.

"Agents, I thought I'd find you here. Saw your SUVs in the lot." Detective McClellan stood at the end of our table.

No sign of Detective Hogan, but I can't say I was really surprised.

"We've got some news." He took in the table and scanned the

immediate area. He spotted a free chair and pulled it over.

"First of all, next of kin was notified and it met with the usual reaction. Denial, anger, and then a bunch of tears." McClellan paused. None of us said anything, so he continued. "With Ellis succumbing to his injuries, needless to say, an autopsy has been arranged for this afternoon. As Hogan had said last night, we believe Ellis was gagged." McClellan pinched his lips and dropped his hand. "They were able to pull a partial print from the small piece of silver tape that we found near his mouth."

"Was there a match?"

The detective shook his head. "Nothing in any database."

"Have it tested for bodily fluids. We might come away with sweat transfer." Jack rhymed off the next course of action, but his words stalled with the detective's smile.

"Already taken care of. Further testing is being done."

This guy was impressive, but it took more than that to excite Jack. "When will we have the results?" he asked.

"If anything comes through on them, I will let you know immediately."

Zachery pushed his plate into the middle of the table. "We're after a guy who doesn't have a record. He's been killing for who knows how long and has never been caught. He's smart."

"This confirms, again, that Bowen isn't our man." The words came without thought. I was just proud that I had called it before anyone else. I noticed the deep contemplation in Jack's eyes. "What are you thinking?"

Jack looked past me to Zachery. "You mentioned our killer is smart. Kent Fields went to an Ivy League university."

"He's won Pulitzers," McClellan chimed in.

"We'll need to find out if he has a truck, or a Nissan, registered to him." I hardly pictured Fields cruising around in either one, but who knows. The man struck me as too flashy to have a pickup or a compact sedan. The only thing that would fit in the scenario was the color red. It would get noticed.

The detective picked up his phone and made the request.

Watching him, I realized something. "I'm doubting the

intelligence aspect."

Everyone turned to me.

"Think of it. He shows up to kidnap Ellis in a bright red car? Why not something more subdued?"

Paige was the first to nod.

"Maybe our killer is a person of limited means?" Zachery said.

"Limited means? It was a newer model, remember, and he has at least two vehicles. I can barely afford one."

"Hmm."

Paige laughed. "So we're looking for a dumb, rich guy?"

"Why not? There are few of those."

"Is he too narcissistic to think that anyone would point him out?"

Zachery shook his head. "No. It would be just the opposite. He'd believe everyone is paying attention to him, and if they were not, they should be."

"So he's wanting to get stopped? Still, the color red for a vehicle used to kidnap someone. In broad daylight? That's pretty brazen."

McClellan hung up his cell, grinning as if the results were going to burst out of him. "Kent Fields owns a truck."

"What about a car?" Jack asked.

The detective's face fell. "Yes, a Mercedes."

"The car could have been a rental." Paige brushed the crumbs from her hands onto her plate.

Jack snapped his fingers and pointed at her. "You go with Zachery to visit that girl right now. We're going to get Fields' prints."

McClellan laughed softly. "You think he's just going to hand them over?"

Jack glowered. "We can be very convincing."

CHAPTER 24

THE ADVOCATE GROUND THE HEELS of his palms into the steering wheel. Patience defined him unless failure entered in. How could the timing have been any more catastrophic? It should have been perfect. He was so absorbed in planning Ellis's execution that he had failed to keep proper tabs on the man who was to take the fall—Bowen.

He had been the ideal candidate. He had a habit of sending hate mail to those who beat animal abuse charges and it had put him on the FBI's radar. He had no doubt Ellis would have received one of those letters. And, while Bowen was a man of like mind, if it came down to one of them being put behind bars, he'd rather it be Bowen. The confinement to a cell would have the Advocate suicidal in days, if it took even that long.

No. He was meant to be free to continue on with his noteworthy mission in life. When he was young, an event had laid the foundation for this, and then, years ago, it had come back to him, assigning him purpose. It was too dominant to be considered anything less than a calling. Bringing justice for the defenseless was the reason he was put on this earth.

The thought made him smile, but it faded with the onset of a nagging conscience. It would do so periodically, rapping away as a woodpecker does against the bark of a tree, the constant rhythm enough to wish oneself deaf.

In the end, his strategy had failed and the person who should have taken the fall, walked free.

He was already working faster than ever before. Up until a

week ago, it had been three murders in twenty-six years, now that number had doubled.

His previous self would have passed judgment, insisting that his moral standards were waning, but the barrier between right and wrong had become a wavy line.

At night when he closed his eyes, he would see those of the Offenders, pleading with him and begging for reprieve. After his first few kills, these recollections had brought a shred of remorse, but he refined his focus. It was by his actions that they had been set free from their sins. He had rebalanced the scales of justice.

Part of him reasoned it would be best to stop for a while, but there was work to be done. And maybe if the feds caught their "killer," he could carry on in silence, at his own pace. But for that to happen, there would be no room for mistakes. He had to cast the light where it belonged or lose everything.

He just wished he had more time to select a winning candidate, but as long as the FBI were searching, he would leave a trail. Only it wouldn't be him they'd find.

CONNIE SHEPARD'S BOYFRIEND OPENED THE DOOR. His bangs stood up as if he had gelled them into place, the spiky do disclosing a night of tossing and turning. The dark crescents under his eyes spoke to a hangover.

"You came back. It's a little early, isn't it?" He rubbed his forehead and dropped his arm to the door knob.

"It's after eight in the morning. Could we speak to Miss Shepard, please," Paige said.

His eyes skimmed over her and passed to Zach. "I'll get her." He stepped away from the front door but left it open. The temperature outside was well below freezing and Paige took it as an invitation to enter the house. Zach followed.

"Hey, what do you want?" A sleepy-eyed Connie Shepard came toward them, dressed in plaid pajamas and white slippers. Her hair was in a haphazard ponytail that left long strands hanging out at the sides.

"We'd like to talk to you about yesterday."

"Of course you would." Her voice was gravelly. "But I'm not sure what I can tell you. I told the cops everything yesterday."

A male was passed out on the couch in front of them. Paige asked Connie, "Do you have some place we can sit and talk?"

"Sure. This way." She led them into the kitchen.

The smell of burnt coffee hung in the air. The table was full of beer bottles, along with an empty bottle of tequila. It had been a good party, and from the look of it, Connie's boyfriend was paying heavily.

Connie slipped onto a kitchen chair, her leg bent beneath her. She settled her gaze on Paige. "I'm not sure what else I can say."

"When you first heard him—"

"I thought it was my grandmother's ghost."

"Why?"

"I dunno." Her lips curled and she adjusted her sitting position.

"The report says that you heard moaning. I'm just curious why you would conclude it was a ghost." Paige leveled eye contact with her, wondering what her response would be to that question.

Connie remained quiet.

"Did your grandmother moan?"

The boyfriend laughed and it warranted a crossway glare from Connie. He was standing next to the counter and held up his hands in surrender.

"No, she didn't moan."

The energy in the room took on a slight shift and held more of a serious tone.

"Is he still alive? The man I found?" Tears beaded in her blue eyes and she studied Paige's.

"He died on the way to the hospital."

A few tears fell down Connie's cheeks.

"Had you seen him before?"

"No."

"So your grandmother—"

"I think he said something."

Paige glanced at Zach. Did Shepard hear him say more than I'm sorry? Paige wasn't going to say a word unless Connie needed more prompting. Sometimes all it took to silence someone was speaking at the wrong time, and it wasn't worth that risk.

"I had a dream last night, surprisingly. I didn't sleep much."

A dog came up to Connie and she ran a hand along its back. He was a big number and heavy with fur.

"Nice dog." Paige smiled. "And he's quiet too."

Connie sniffled. "She's a good girl. She's my joy." She continued rubbing at the back of the dog's neck.

The motion made Paige wonder if the girl would feel any sympathy for the man she found fighting for life on the side of the road if she knew his history.

"He's a Bernese Mountain dog," Zachery said.

"That's right." Connie smiled, seemingly impressed by his knowledge.

"What's her name?"

She laughed. "Roxie. She's six." Another rub had Roxie looking up at Connie, panting and flashing a doggie smile.

"You mentioned you had a dream," Paige said.

Connie pried her eyes from Roxie. "Yeah, but I think it was more of a memory. All I could see was myself walking down that road. And then that man in the ditch. His voice was muffled and carried on the wind, but I think he said something about a key."

A good night's sleep—and possibly the alcohol—had jarred Connie's memory.

"Key?" Zach asked.

Connie nodded, but there was no conviction in her eyes.

"Did he say anything else?"

"Yeah," Connie's attention went to Roxie, who had settled into a ball at her feet, "stupid kid." Connie lifted her head and shrugged. "That's what he first said and why I thought it was my grandmother."

CHAPTER 25

THE MAN AT THE FRONT desk of Fields' condo building frowned when he saw us. "You're back."

There wasn't even an attempt at geniality.

It didn't deter Jack. "Kent Fields in?"

"That would violate his privacy." He pronounced it like '*privicy*' as if he were of English background.

Jack spoke through clenched teeth. "If you don't answer, you're interfering with an open investigation, and that means charges and jail time."

The man's hands went to the counter and he splayed his fingers. His gaze fell behind us and then met with my eyes. "He's away."

"When did you last see him?" I asked.

"Last night."

"And how did he seem to you?"

"Is he in trouble?"

"Don't know yet." Jack held eye contact. The man looked away first.

"He seemed rushed. He usually wipes his feet on the front mat," he pointed to it, "but he didn't. I had to call in the janitor to mop up behind him. He left pools of melted snow on the floor. Something like that would open us up to a lawsuit if someone slipped and fell."

"What time was that?"

"Eight-ish."

That would fit in with the timeframe. "When did he leave?"

"Say, fifteen minutes later, if that. I know because the janitor bitched when he saw him again. Of course, not in front of Fields."

"Of course not," Jack said dryly. "Was he packed to go somewhere?"

"Nah. I don't think so. Just in a hurry, like something bad had happened and he had to get somewhere."

Jack was already on the move. He must have been thinking the same thing as me—Fields could be on the run.

I caught up with him, regretting it as soon as I hit the cold air. I wasn't sure how people who lived here did it. It was below zero for five months of the year, or maybe that was a myth, like all Canadians play hockey and live in igloos—then again, maybe they did. I had never lived in Canada.

"Should we call this in?" I asked. "Fields left here about the time we figured Ellis was dragged. He appeared upset. Heck, probably because he had just sentenced a man to death."

Jack pulled out a cigarette and lit up. He had the process down to a fine art and could do it in seconds.

"What would make Fields risk everything?" I asked.

"The why isn't something we always get answered."

I continued on with my line of thought. "He's at the top of the publishing industry. People want to be him."

"People have risked a lot before. Their drive moves them to do things that are beyond reason."

Jack stopped walking and stood in the middle of the lot.

"I don't know if I'm buying it or not," I said.

I let seconds tick off as I thought about where we stood. There were few viable suspects. Bowen, who seemed to have the strongest motivation, was cleared. Fields was the next closest person to these cases. He would have intimate knowledge from interviews with the clinics where the animals were brought in. We should never have cut him loose. We should have at least brought him in for intense questioning.

"The records show that Fields has two vehicles, right? So even if he's gone, he can only drive one."

"Hmm."

"We could let ourselves into the underground parking lot and see if, by chance, his truck is there." It was a long shot. If Fields had dragged Ellis with his truck that would be the vehicle he fled in, but I was already on the move toward the garage.

There were two motorized rolling steel doors—one for entry and one for exit. It required a passkey. I was about to turn to Jack for *the what's next* when a door lifted.

Jack and I held up our credentials to the driver, who didn't even seem to care while we squeezed between their car and the garage door's frame. It was disappointing actually. I thought we'd at least get into it with a guard or a valet. There weren't even other tenants around.

I pointed to painted numbers on the walls. "Each spot has an assigned unit."

"It also looks like every unit gets only one spot."

"It's possible the penthouse gets two. Bigger bucks, greater privileges."

We had walked around for a few minutes before we spotted the word *Penthouse*. If that didn't place a target on a man's back to have his car keyed, I'm not sure what would. A two-door Mercedes was parked in the space.

I stated the obvious. "And his truck is missing."

Jack already had his cell to his ear. "Get an APB out on Fields and his pickup immediately."

My stomach tightened and I wondered if we'd had our killer but had let him go. Maybe it didn't matter to Fields that he risked everything. Maybe he had concluded that creating justice, albeit his own warped version, was tantamount in importance, even to his freedom.

Jack's face took on hardened lines as he stomped out his cigarette on the concrete. Based on his reaction, he was getting some news too.

CHAPTER 26

JACK AND I HELD UP our creds and brushed past the officer at the front door of Clyde Ellis's house.

"Hey, hold on there. You can't just go in." The officer raised his arms in frustration. "At least give me your names."

"Last names, Harper and Fisher," I called back to him, still on the move forward.

We found Detective McClellan in the living room with one hand on his hip, the other holding a file. His eyes were contemplative.

"Have we found any evidence against Fields?" Jack asked.

McClellan shook his head. "Not yet, but the APB has been issued, as you requested."

"Hmm."

The detective looked from Jack to me as if seeking an explanation for Jack's guttural sound. I had worked by Jack's side for months and still wasn't an expert at its interpretation.

I filled McClellan in on the details. "Fields was seen last night about eight, by the front desk clerk in his building. He described Fields as being in a hurry and not his usual self. It turns out his truck is missing, and all we know is that he had a connection with our two dead victims and the three missing men. As for the truck, we also searched the above-ground lot just in case he had parked it there for some reason, but there was no sign of it."

"So, he drags Ellis, leaves him to die, and then makes a run for it. Seems quite possible to me." McClelland bobbed his head side to side.

"We still haven't got a definite motive, but sometimes we don't get those right away. We know that he wrote those pieces and would have had access to the abused animals, but was it enough to push him over—"

"Stop. Get back here." The officer from the front door followed Paige and Zachery as far as the living room.

McClellan waved the officer back. "They're fine, Cross."

"Tell us more about the circumstances surrounding the charges against Ellis," Jack said.

"Well, he was coming down off of a high when he was found. He kept saying, 'It won't stop barking.'"

"The dog deserved it for barking?" I shook my head. The thought made me sick.

"Apparently, and, sadly, it ended up dying."

"Unbelievable." Paige knotted her arms, her eyes intent and raging.

I'm sure we were all feeling the same way. It was hard to sympathize with a man who afflicted such cruelty on an animal. It spurred a feeling of comradery toward the killer, who was repaying these men in kind. But our job wasn't to pass judgment. We had to stop him.

"Have you come across any hate mail?" Zachery asked.

"Nothing so far."

"We pulled prints from the doorbell, but who knows, the guy could have knocked. Maybe the door was unlocked and he came right in. And before you ask, no clear prints came back from the door handle," McClellan said, directing his last statement to Jack.

Paige slipped her hands into her back pockets. "I'm thinking it might be a good idea to cross compare any prints you pull to the hate mail received by Lyons. It's possible we could find a link there."

"I can do that."

"What would push Fields to this point?" I asked, trying to reestablish brainstorming.

"Like we touched on, he had firsthand knowledge of these cases. He was probably reporting on them not long after they took place," Zachery said. "He could have even been around the abused animals."

"Meaning that he could have witnessed the animal's suffering. I can't imagine seeing that." Paige crossed her arms and rocked left to right, right to left. "Our killer could have also had a pet in the past that was abused or mistreated. Most likely in his formative years, between the ages of seven to ten."

"Well, if we can't find Fields, we know who the next closest person would be," Jack said.

"He has three living relatives, Boss—his father, Bowen, and his mother."

"Start with Bowen. Question him about their childhood."

"Their parents got together when they were fifteen and sixteen. It could go back further than that," Zach offered.

"Zach's right, Boss," Paige stated.

"It's possible that Bowen hasn't been asked the right question."

Silence fell and our attention went to Detective McClellan. It was as if we all realized that he had called us here but hadn't yet given us his reason.

I pointed to the folder in his hand. "Detective, is that why you had us hurry over?"

"Ah. Yes, it is." He held up the file. "This is the deceased's Will and Power of Attorney, but it's only a copy. He left a handwritten note that if he died of suspicious means that his lawyer had more information."

"Lawyer's name and address?"

"E Nagy and Associates, and the law firm's just downtown."

"Brandon and I've got this." Jack pointed a finger at Paige and Zachery. "You two talk to Bowen and push him hard about his stepbrother's childhood. See if he has any idea where he might be. And yes, Zach, I know they weren't close. It's still worth a try. McClellan, you have my cell. Update us immediately if you find anything else."

CHAPTER 27

CRAIG BOWEN OPENED THE DOOR dressed in a pair of jogging pants and a Budweiser t-shirt. "What are you doing here?"

Even when Bowen was brought in, Paige and Zach never met him face to face. They must have "the look." Either way, he knew they were FBI.

"I'm not really sure who you feds think you are. You drag me downtown, after coming at me like the cavalry, and what's that? That's right. I'm an innocent man. I've wasted enough of my life on this bullshit."

"We're here about your stepbrother," Zach said.

Bowen had started to inch the door shut but stopped. "What do you want with Kent? Is he all right?"

Paige smiled, doing her best to use her female charm. "Can we come in?"

Bowen rolled his eyes and stepped back.

"Do you have somewhere we can sit down?"

"Would you like me to put on a pot of coffee and grab some biscuits? Actually," Bowen snapped his fingers, "I never got to my baking today. What a shame. If only I knew you were coming." He slipped onto the sofa and adjusted some throw pillows. "You think he's behind the murders now?"

Paige was fascinated how the man seemed to have an entire conversation with himself before coming back around to the reason they were there. "He's missing." She spoke the words matter-of-factly, hoping that it would impress the urgency of the situation.

Bowen didn't say anything.

"Another man was murdered. Your brother—"

"Stepbrother."

"Stepbrother—who you seemed awfully concerned about just a few seconds ago." She played on his sarcasm.

"Really, he's a big boy and can take care of himself."

"We're hoping that you might know where Kent could be, know of any places he liked to go."

Bowen laughed and wiped his lips, lingering there as if removing food residue.

"We know you weren't close. But maybe you can remember where he liked to go when he was younger?"

A smirk lifted Bowen's lips but didn't touch his eyes. "You really think he did this?"

"We can't answer that in so many words."

"You just did." Bowen paused for a bit and seemed to consider whether or not to share his thoughts. "He liked to go to Railyard Dog Park. He found being around the animals peaceful, and he'd write in a stupid journal and talk about the day he'd prove himself to all of us." When Bowen caught Paige's eye, he said, "Guess he did."

Zach picked up his cell and dialed in what they were just told.

Bowen pointed to him and spoke to Paige. "Kent was always a self-obsessed person, but murder? I'm not too sure."

"That's the thing with killers, Mr. Bowen. A lot of times they seem like regular people."

Zach hung up and informed Paige. "They're sending cars to that location."

Bowen edged forward on the couch. "Is he going to be okay?"

Paige found the question odd. Why was he suddenly worried about his stepbrother, who, moments earlier, he had distanced himself from by reminding them they don't share the same blood.

"Did you have a family pet while growing up? A cat? A dog?"

"Nope. Mother was allergic."

"What about Kent and his father, before they moved in with you?"

Bowen's face screwed upward. "Come to think of it, he did have a dog. Can't remember the breed. It was small but quite the hairball. Mother definitely wouldn't have been all right with it."

"So he had to let his dog go?"

"I remember him saying Checkers went to heaven."

"Checkers?"

"Yeah, it was black and white, so it made perfect sense. Anyway, I think it was a Lhasa apso."

"He went to heaven?" Paige slid her glance to Zach. "Convenient timing."

"Do you think his dad killed the dog?" Bowen asked. There was evidence of anger in his eyes and his leg was bouncing. "How am I supposed to help find justice against these creeps when I can't even recognize an animal abuser when I see one? I lived with him until graduation."

Paige realized how that would come as a blow to a man who'd dedicated his spare time to an activist group that spoke out about that very thing.

Bowen stood and formed fists at his side. "I'm going to—"

"Violence is not the answer."

A red-faced Bowen fixed his gaze on Paige. "Sometimes it is."

Zach moved beside Bowen. "Are you threatening harm against Kent's father?"

As the two men locked eyes, Paige picked up on the underlying communication. Bowen's instinct was to exact revenge, but he didn't want to go back to jail. He broke the eye contact.

Zach kept watching him. "You know that if anything happens to the man, we'll be coming right back here. With cuffs. You won't be walking away."

Bowen nodded.

"All right." Zach paused for a few seconds and got up. Paige followed his lead.

"Let me know if you find him," Bowen called out to them.

Chapter 28

I did a double take of the name on the side of the building. Typically, signs for law firms consisted of long, uncommon, hard-to-pronounce names, but these ones actually inspired a smile.

Ellis's lawyer was Elbert Nagy. It was one thing to have heard his name, which is pronounced like *Nawdge* rhyming with dodge, but quite another to see it in large brass lettering. It did not read at all the way it sounded.

The receptionist was a trim brunette who smiled when we walked in the front door.

"Welcome to E Nagy and Associates. How may I assist you today?"

The words flowed from her mouth with ease. She had been at this post for a long time and the experience was evident. Even when the smile faded, her face was relaxed and pleasant. She enjoyed her position. And I figured, based on the office decor, got paid handsomely to greet people, answer phones, and type up letters.

"FBI Special Agents Fisher and Harper. We have an appointment to see Mr. Nagy." The name was even stranger to say. My American brain wanted to pronounce it *Nag-ee*.

"Certainly. One moment, please." She held a pen perched in her left hand as she pressed a button on her headset. "Mr. Nagy, the FBI are here to see you."

I noticed how she didn't give any reaction to the FBI meeting with her boss. Her paycheck much have covered discretion too. It made sense when all it would take was the wrong reaction to forfeit a potential client. Lawyers were a dime a dozen, so they needed to be competitive and customer-service oriented as well.

She touched her headset again. "Sherry, can you please show a couple of clients in for a meeting with Mr. Nagy." There was a pause, followed by a professional-sounding *thank you*. The receptionist's focus went back to us. "Sherry will be up to escort you back shortly. If you would like to have a seat, please feel welcome to. Would you like a cup of fresh coffee while you wait? A Christmas cookie from Lynn's? I wouldn't pass that one up." She extended a silver tray loaded with the confection. It had me wondering how many people went through the place in a day.

Jack waved his hand to dismiss her offer. I accepted even though I wasn't sure why. I certainly didn't need the carbs. Tonight I'd have to hit the hotel gym to get rid of the caloric intake.

"Coffee?"

Her question caught me with my mouth full. I chewed quickly and swallowed. "I'm good. Thank you."

Jack passed a glance from me to the cookies, to the receptionist. Let him think what he wanted. I wasn't the first man to take a treat from a pretty woman.

"What nationality is Nagy?" I asked the receptionist.

She smiled politely, excused herself for a minute, answered and directed a call, and then came back to my question. "Nagy is a common Hungarian surname."

I nodded as if she were confirming a suspicion, but the truth was I had no idea of its background. "I bet you get that question a lot."

"Yes." She grinned again, and this time there was more behind the eyes. I better slow things down or I'd be dead times two—first by Jack, and then Paige would have her turn.

"Mr. Harper and Mr. Fisher?" A redhead dressed in a pencil skirt and white blouse came toward us. She was thin enough that I wondered if she'd disappear if she turned sideways. Her footwear wasn't made for comfort, the heels were at least three inches high with a slender spike. I wouldn't want to get on her bad side and earn a kick in the shins that was for certain. I imagined she slipped out of them the moment she got home, to let the arch of her feet relax.

We followed her to a conference room, where she indicated for us to go inside. I had anticipated that we would be shown to Nagy's office, but it was apparent that the man preferred to keep it private from clients. At least from us.

"Mr. Harper? Fisher?" A man in his late fifties stood from the head of the table. He buttoned up his suit jacket and came at us with an extended hand. "I'm Mr. Nagy. Sherry, please close the door for us."

"Certainly." She smiled pleasantly like the receptionist had, and it had me speculating if it was included in their job descriptions.

After the door had clicked shut, Mr. Nagy spoke. "Please, take a seat wherever you'd like. I'm used to sitting at the head of the table if you don't mind, but otherwise…"

Jack and I both took a seat near Nagy at the end of the table.

Nagy's eyes were dark and deeply set. His build was solid, neither thin nor overweight, and he was about five ten. The suit he wore spoke of a sizable investment, but I didn't wager it was Armani.

"I understand you're here to discuss Clyde Ellis." He clasped his hands on top of a file folder that was on the table. A pair of glasses was beside it. "I cannot discuss a client's personal information. I'm sure you understand."

"Mr. Ellis is dead," Jack said.

"Oh?"

It was the single-worded inquiry, which had been used as a successful trolling expedition for many decades, centuries even, for a reason—it worked.

"He was murdered."

"Oh." He dragged out the word this time.

There was something about the way his eyes lit and the way the word took on a deep tone. "You don't seem surprised," I said.

"Well, that's probably because I'm not."

"Why aren't you?" Jack asked.

Nagy's lips pressed and he shook his head. "I'm sorry, but I cannot discuss this with you unless you have a warrant. Even in death, the client has rights. I'm sure you under—"

There was a knock on the door.

"Come in." Irritation coated Nagy's voice.

Sherry entered and handed Nagy a few sheets of paper.

He took the pair of glasses from the table and put them on. He read the document, his lips moving as he did so. He lowered his glasses as well as the paper. "Well, it seems you have your warrant." He waved his girl away and when she was gone, he spoke. "I would still like to see the original warrant, but will still help you out now."

"Mr. Ellis's file." Jack extended his hand.

Nagy's hand held a slight tremor as he passed it over.

"Is there something you should be telling us?" I asked.

He folded up his glasses and held them in his hand. "Mr. Ellis thought he might be murdered."

My mind went back to McClellan's words. *He left a handwritten note that if he died of suspicious means that his lawyer had more information.*

Nagy continued. "He was in a real hurry when he set out to do his Will. That was twenty-six years ago. I haven't seen him since, but he left explicit instructions about what was to be done, 'if or when' he was murdered. Who even knows if it works anymore?"

"It?" Jack took a white envelope from the file and opened it. A key dropped into his palm, along with a small piece of lined paper.

I remembered what Paige had said Connie Shepard told her. She said that she heard Ellis mention a key.

Jack passed the note to me.

The text was handwritten in blue ink and read *"If I'm murdered. This is the key to my killer. Colorado Vault & Safe Deposit Box Co."*

CHAPTER 29

WE UPDATED PAIGE AND ZACHERY that we were headed to Colorado Vault & Safe in Centennial, which was a small town about half an hour away. The obvious conclusion was the key belonged to a safety deposit box numbered twenty-three eighty-four, as inscribed on the key, assuming it was still rented by Ellis. The lawyer had mentioned it was left with him twenty-six years ago.

The warrant went through and covered all legal paperwork and the contents of the box. We were directed to a small room and told to wait a few minutes.

"Here you go." A middle-aged man handed us a box.

Jack took it from him. "When was Mr. Ellis last here, and please confirm when the box was first taken out."

"I can certainly find out for you."

Jack didn't respond with a nod, a smile, or a thank you. His energy communicated that we'd be waiting and the man was to advise us as soon as possible.

The man left and closed the door behind him.

Jack opened the container, and inside there were numerous envelopes of all different sizes and colors.

"The hate mail." The obvious observation left my mouth without thought. Jack stopped removing items to give me his you're-a-genius look.

I pulled out a tri-folded piece of paper. It was on its own, not enclosed in an envelope, and it garnered my attention. It was a handwritten letter by Ellis.

"If you are reading this, I'm dead. Someone has killed

me. Or, at least, I suspect so. And it was probably at the hand of one of the people who wrote a letter. People hated me for what I did to Benjamin. I don't even remember all of it. At least, not clearly. I know he just wouldn't stop barking and it gave me a pounding headache. I probably wanted to give him a headache."

"This guy deserved what he got, Jack. I'd say sorry for thinking that, but I'm not. Who can hurt an animal, not care if they even killed it and feel the action was justified?"

"Keep reading."

I studied his eyes for a bit before returning to the letter. The issue ate away at him too, the conflict that was apparent in this case—we had to hold a killer responsible even if his motives seemed noble.

"Turns out, I gave Benjamin more than a headache. They don't expect him to survive. What have I done? But it's done. I can't reverse it. I blame the cocaine…coming down from it. I will never touch the stuff again!

"And to think I got away with it…maybe I do deserve to die.

"I am going to work at becoming a changed man. I was forgiven this time…or was I? And it's all because I was after a high. Stupid kid."

Paige had told us Connie Sheppard heard Ellis say the exact same thing. *Stupid kid.*

There was a soft knock on the door.

"Come in," Jack said.

"The box was taken out twenty-six years ago, almost to the day. The only time he was here, according to the records, is the day he took out the box."

"Is there any way he could access it without there being a record?" I asked.

"No, absolutely not. Just like you had to sign in, Mr. Ellis would have been required to as well."

"And there's no way the record keeping would fail?"

The bank employee's mouth contorted as if he were thinking of saying one thing but opted for another. "No."

Maybe I was being difficult, but I found it interesting that Ellis would take out the box twenty-six years ago and never revisit it. Although, maybe his feelings of guilt had held him back.

"Okay, thank you."

He left the room and I turned to Jack, who was tapping his shirt pocket for a cigarette.

I was beginning to recognize it as an automatic impulse Jack had when he was stressed or didn't like the direction a case was going. He also seemed to do it when we were narrowing in on closing an investigation. I dismissed my analysis. He was just an addict, plain and simple.

"So, Ellis took out the box and never came back," I said.

"Seems to me he no longer felt threatened."

"I was thinking the same thing at first. Except why hold onto the box? Why not get rid of it?"

Jack and I remained silent for a few seconds. With the quiet came the revelation that I had on the tip of my brain yesterday morning at breakfast. My heart raced.

"Jack, the bartender commented on Simpson and how he only went with friends he had known for a long time." I paused, welcoming a verbal acknowledgment, but he said nothing and didn't even give any visual indication he was listening. "To keep the box, Ellis thought the threat against him was still alive, but if he suspected a specific person he would have updated the contents with their name. He didn't."

"Hmm."

I took that one as a good sign and went on. "Also, it didn't seem that Ellis was under distress when he got into the Nissan with the other man, who we assume is our killer."

The reflection in his eyes told me he understood where I was headed.

"Our unsub isn't a stranger to the people he's killing. They may very well know him."

CHAPTER 30

THE TEAM WAS BACK AT the field office discussing everything we had found out.

"We got the name of a park from Bowen, but there was no sign of Fields," Paige said.

Zachery was across the table from me, his hands wrapped around a coffee mug. "He said that Fields had a dog before he and his father moved in with them. Bowen's mother was allergic."

"But that's not the interesting part." Paige's eyes lit up. "Apparently the dog went to heaven not long before that. Good timing or orchestrated?"

"You're thinking that this may have been the traumatic event that left Fields wanting to take revenge on these dog abusers," Jack concluded.

"It's possible," Zachery said. "We also put a car on Fields' father's address. No sign of Fields there either."

"If it was his father who basically started all this, why wait so long and why not just go straight to the father?" I asked.

Zachery considered my question for a second. "He may be building his way up to his ultimate target."

"With us watching over his dad, he'll never show up."

"The kid's got a point. Make sure that it's an unmarked car and they allow some space."

"Jack? Are you sure you want to do that? It doesn't take long to kill someone."

There was a fire in Jack's eyes when he glared at Paige. "We have to bait Fields."

"How do you propose we do that?" I asked.

It met with no response.

Paige picked up her cell to contact Denver PD with their revised approach plan. She hung up seconds later. "Done. They'll hang back."

"We're still waiting on Nadia to finish working through the bar receipts. That needs to be rushed." I thought I'd take a stab from another direction.

"And she still needs to update me about the politicians in the area from twenty-six years ago," Paige said.

Jack glanced at me. "The kid had a good idea."

On first instinct, I hated the nickname being in there, but the compliment faded its negative impact.

"He had the idea that maybe our killer isn't a stranger to the men he's targeting."

"Interesting thought, Pending."

Did Zachery think I needed his praise?

"Wait. Didn't Jenna Simpson mention that her husband had a new friend he was spending time with?" Paige asked me.

"Yeah, a woman, remember? We have no reason to think our killer is a female."

"No, like we've concluded before, it's a male, based on victimology. He only kills men. A female wouldn't hesitate to kill either sex," Zachery said. "She'd exact vengeance on both."

Paige laughed. "Remember that when you cross me, guys."

Jack even smiled at that comment, but the expression was short-lived and he went back to business. "What else have we got?"

"It looks like Ellis had a bit of a gambling problem. His financial reports correspond with the past due bills found in his home. The guy was broke. More than broke. It seemed the only person getting paid was the lawyer. Besides the security box and bills to keep a roof over his head, everything else was in arrears."

"What about the letters Brandon and I brought in from Ellis's safety deposit box?" Jack asked.

Zachery spun his mug. "No update on the results at this point, from a forensic side of things. However, I've read all of them, including the ones received from Lyons. A lot of them were similar. Like the same people sent them out for all instances of animal abuse charges. There is one, though, that got my attention. Even more so after realizing Ellis received the exact same letter. While most of them didn't hold back from describing how justice was going to be worked out, these letters merely read 'You will pay for what you have done.'"

"If this is from our unsub, he's shown a lot of patience." My statement made me realize something. I sat up straighter. "What if Ball and Garner weren't the first?"

"You're forgetting that we checked into that already. Nothing came up, Kid."

"Maybe we're just missing something."

Paige leaned forward on the table and clasped her hands. "Let's go with the theory he bided his time. He isn't an impulsive killer. He does a lot of planning and doesn't act on a whim. Each murder is premeditated. With Kent Fields, his career was just getting started. Reporting on these cases could have brought back what his father had done to their dog. He was angered, but willing to take his time in exacting revenge."

"Like you said he's not a natural killer. He was triggered."

"Exactly."

"And he was triggered by what?"

"We need to figure that out," Jack said.

"There are only two other missing people before Lyons. Dean Garner, the first reported, only dates back to two thousand nine," Zachery said.

"And he was charged with what again?" Paige asked.

"It's a good thing for my wonderful memory, isn't it?" Zachery smiled and received a playful glare from Paige. "He was charged with neglect. He had left the family dog, outside on a hot day. There was a heat advisory. The dog's heart failed."

"Gene Lyons left his dog unattended and tied, with a choker of all things, to a back deck. It strangled itself," I said. "A coincidence or a pattern? Maybe this is what Fields' father was guilty of? Then again, Simpson used poison."

"Okay, but, going back to Garner. He was married, right? Seems I have a memory too." Paige paused to flash a sardonic smile at Zachery. "His wife reported him missing after deciding enough time had passed and her husband should be home. Sounds like she's a couch potato who doesn't have much of a life. She's just as responsible for what happened to the dog as her husband."

"Yeah, she's probably still well and alive."

"Exactly, Brandon." She bit her bottom lip. "Our killer is really fixated on male abusers who get away with it."

"By the sounds of it, possibly just like Fields' father, assuming he did play a part in the dog's death."

"All right. It's time to pay Garner's wife a visit." Jack pulled out a cigarette. "Paige and Zach you go there. Brandon and I are going to talk to Fields' father."

Chapter 31

JILL GARNER MOVED ABOUT THE living room of her home, picking up stuffed toys. Most she threw into a toy chest at the side of the room, but she kept a hold on a loosely stuffed bear. She played with its ears as she spoke. "My husband was a decent man."

Paige had to wonder about how *decent* either of them were. Where was Jill when the dog was melting on the back deck?

Jill's three-year-old granddaughter, Denise, sat at her feet playing with a Barbie. She was moving its arms and legs, and would periodically grab it by the hair and sway it side to side.

"The file notes that your husband was gone for three days before you reported him. I take it your husband was often gone?" Paige asked.

She kept tugging on the bear's ear. "He was a—" She let go of the toy and held up a hand to shelter her granddaughter from seeing her—as if she'd know how to spell at her age. She mouthed, "D-r-u-n-k."

"And that didn't bother you?"

"Of course it did, but what was I supposed to do about it? Leave him? He brought in the money. I had to get a job, thanks to him up and disappearing."

Paige's face heated. The woman had been around while the dog suffered. She glanced at the little girl. It was time that she left the room. She looked at Jill. "Is there a room where Denise can go play while we talk?"

The implication registered in Jill's eyes. The subject matter was about to get a lot darker.

"Deni, why don't I get you a juice and you can watch *Aladdin* in Grandma's room?"

Her blue eyes lit and widened. "Okay." The Barbie was tossed aside and forgotten.

When Jill returned, she no longer had the bear, and Paige surmised it got left behind with Denise to watch the movie.

"I've heard about what's been happening around here lately. Those men who were murdered. The paper is hinting toward a serial killer targeting animal abusers from nearly three decades ago. Do you think this same person took Dean?"

"It's too early to say for sure, but we suspect it may be a possibility. Do you know this man?" Zach extended a photograph of Kent Fields.

She took it and studied it briefly. "He looks familiar. He's someone famous, isn't he?"

"He's an award-winning journalist."

"Ah, probably why I recognize him." She handed the photo back to Zach.

"Was your husband friends with him, or ever mention him?"

"No." She slid her eyes from Zachery to Paige. "Should he have?"

"What about any new friends in your husband's life around the time he went missing?"

Jill patted the arms of the chair. "You never answered my question, but I'm supposed to answer yours?"

"We don't know if they were friends, we're trying to find that out," Paige said.

Satisfied, Jill continued. "No, I don't remember mention of any new friends, but who knows."

"What about hate mail after the charges were laid against your husband?"

"Oh, now you're stretching my mind to twenty-some years ago, but I think so."

"You must not have taken them very seriously."

"People spout things off all the time. It doesn't mean they are going to act on them."

"You wouldn't still have them around, would you?"

Jill laughed. "Heavens, no. And at this point, I couldn't even tell you any names that were on the letters. Although, I think one was from the animal activist group, Humanity Against Animal Abusers."

CHAPTER 32

SHANE FIELDS WAS AN OLDER VERSION OF KENT. His eyes were a brilliant blue and stood out in contrast to his light complexion. His eyebrows were nearly white with a tinge of blond while the hair on his head was mostly gray.

He lived in an esteemed neighborhood and the house made me think of Jenna Simpson's.

Shane hesitated to let us in, but eventually did and led us into his living room.

"Why are you interested in Kent?" he asked, as he lowered into a stiff-looking reading chair. He directed us to a matching sofa.

"Before we get into that, we have some questions about his childhood," Jack said.

Shane angled his head. "I don't understand why that would interest the FBI."

It was apparent we'd have to provide this man more information to get him to open up.

"You've heard about the murdered men in the news, I'm sure."

Shane didn't say anything, or nod. If it wasn't for his rapt attention on Jack, I wouldn't even be sure he heard what Jack had said.

"Your son is a suspect."

Shane's face paled to a point I wouldn't have imagined possible. He sat up straighter, pulling himself upright using the arms of the chair. "You're telling me that my son killed those men?"

"I said he's a suspect."

"And why would that be the case?"

"We believe it all began with a childhood event—"

"Stop right there. I'm not going to allow you to come into my home and tell me that I raised a killer. And that I'm who made him that?" A tint of color was back in the man's cheeks.

"We aren't saying that. Your son reported on cases of animal abuse when his career started out."

"That makes him the killer?" Shane glanced at me. "This is insane."

"Do you know where you son is?"

"Excuse me?"

I was thinking the same thing. Jack had diverted the conversation with a sharp turn.

"He seems to be on the run."

"Or missing?" Shane glowered. "Maybe the real killer has him."

The angles of Jack's features sharpened.

"I have no idea. We're not really close." The last sentence was spoken in a lower volume.

"Yet you're certain he isn't a killer."

Sometimes I wondered if Jack said things to elicit a reaction.

"He bought me this house after his first Pulitzer. Said it was for raising him. It's ironic how many parents give their kids money and gifts to offset being absent from their lives, and here, my son did that to me. Just thought of it that way."

"We understand that you had a dog when Kent was young."

"Yes, a Lhasa apso. Furry thing. This one shed like crazy and had a wild grin. Its bottom teeth protruded over the top."

"What happened to it?"

"It died," he looked between us and added, "of natural causes."

"It was convenient timing with moving in with Bowen's mother," I said. "She had allergies and didn't want the dog."

"You think I killed the dog? That Kent knew about it? And then what? He became traumatized and is taking it out on other people? Is that why I've noticed a squad car outside my house more than once?"

Apparently we had been too late in giving the updated direction to PD to hang back.

Shane's arrogance gave way to a nervous expression. "You think he might come after me?"

"We think it might be a possibility," Jack said. "But if you had nothing to do with the dog's death then—"

"I never killed that damned dog. It was already dying from heart failure. Kids don't realize this, but dogs don't live forever. Checkers was eleven and had a heart murmur from the time she was a pup. I told Kent she went to heaven. In reality, heaven cost me a fortune."

I stated the obvious. "You never killed the dog, but that's not how a young boy might see things. To him, you could have been responsible for its death."

"Ridiculous. There was nothing that I could be done for it."

"Where did you have it put down?" Jack asked.

Shane pushed into his chair. "Paws and Claws Veterinary Clinic. Check it out if you have to." Shane's jaw slid askew. "Now, is that all?"

"One more question for you. Do you know of any places your son might go to get away from things?"

Shane shook his head. "Like I said, we haven't been real close. I know he liked Railyard Dog Park when he was young."

"We've been there and there's no sign of him."

"Well, I don't know what else to say."

Jack's cell phone rang.

"Thank you for your time, Mr. Fields." I stood up and so did Shane.

Jack stayed seated and answered his phone.

Shane passed Jack an odd glance, impatience blanketing over his features. He wanted his solitude back.

"And you're certain?" Jack asked his caller. His eyes latched with mine. He nodded, obviously in response to the answer he was receiving.

It was as if a stone weight had been cast into my stomach—the caller didn't bear good news.

Jack put the phone down and addressed Shane. "Please have a seat." Jack glimpsed at me, but I had a feeling what he had to say.

Shane complied and did as Jack directed.

"We've found your son."

That's all it took—four words.

Shane's face contorted. His chin quivered and he covered his mouth.

"There was an accident and—"

Shane let out a moan of grief and his hand shook.

"He died at the scene. We are sorry for your loss."

The sadness that had stamped all of Shane's features was replaced by a veil of anger. "You thought my son was a killer and now he's dead." He shot to his feet, his face a bright red, and his pointed finger thrust toward the door. "Get out of my house!"

CHAPTER 33

WITH EACH STRIDE, I EXHALED all the negative energy that threatened to swallow me whole. This afternoon had been one of the toughest notifications I had ever been a part of, and I wasn't even the one who delivered the message. I suspected it wouldn't matter if it were my hundredth time—it would still bring with it the same substantive blow.

Kent Fields had been confirmed dead on scene about three hours away from Denver. He was on the way to his lover's bedside. Henry had been rushed in for emergency heart surgery and Kent had wanted to be there for him. By the time he'd arrived, his friend had gone into cardiac arrest and died.

Responders on scene found a bottle of whiskey in Fields' lap. Two-thirds of it was gone.

The only comfort from the sad story was that Fields didn't take anyone else out along with him.

I increased the treadmill's speed and elevation. With each increment it beeped as if warning me, but I welcomed the exertion. Sweat ran down my back and my muscles strained.

The classic rock coming through my earbuds fed my soul, its beat propelling each step. Its message, which alluded to freedom and the ability to be promiscuous without consequence, had Paige entering my mind. She merged with memories of my wife.

I upped the incline.

Purge the negative.

Even with the thought, I had to find a balance, a compromise between releasing the memories and appreciating them for what they were. Right now, the wound was still too fresh. People talk about divorce as if it's not a big deal, it's a natural stage one advances to after marrying. It was almost up there with the getting married and having a baby—an expected conclusion. In that sense, I didn't disappoint. By the time we headed home, I'd be a free man.

Free…there was a concept. Something people longed for all the time but once they tasted supposed freedom, usually they would exchange it for some restriction. Restriction confirmed someone cared about you. Maybe I was crazy for expecting more out of my life.

Tingles pulsed through my arms and face. My heart rate was getting too high. I returned the settings to where they had been.

Paige stepped in front of the treadmill, her mouth forming the word, *Hello?* The arch of a question was implied by the aggravation that was written on her face and the way her brow pushed up in irritation.

I took out my earbuds and smiled. "Couldn't hear you."

"I figured that." She let her eyes scan over me. "What's up?"

"What do you mean? I'm working out."

She smiled the kind that told me she realized there was more to this than trying to work off extra calories.

I stepped to the side plates, straddling the tread, and hit stop. "Rough day."

"Yeah, it was."

I realized then that she wasn't in workout wear. "What's up with you?"

She ran her hands down the front of her thighs. She had paired blue jeans with a cream colored knitted sweater that had her belonging beside a fireplace sipping on red wine.

"What do you mean? The outfit? You don't like it?"

The spark in her eyes had me getting off the treadmill and walking around to meet her. "We can't get caught."

"I know."

I looked past her, around her, and behind myself. No one was in sight.

I cupped her chin and angled her face upward and took her

mouth. For the brief time we were connected, all the negativity melted away. I could have remained in that moment forever.

Her eyes were still closed when I pulled away. They opened slowly, regret filling them.

"I'll have to change first, but do you want to go have a drink?" I asked.

She licked her lips and it had me wanting to do the same. She was savoring my taste and I didn't want to let hers go either.

THE HOTEL'S BAR WAS QUIET and I figured it had more to do with the vicinity of the hotel than the hour. It was only nearing midnight.

We sat in a quiet, dimly lit corner, having passed other couples who were too caught up in their drinks, and each other, to pay us any attention. I wondered how many of them were with their mates and not their mistress. My guess was none of the ones here. The hunger emanating from each of them was tangible. They were here for a forbidden rendezvous.

The waitress took our drink orders and I looked across the table at Paige. She was beautiful in any light, both physically and as a human being. I knew her better than I did myself. At least I thought I did.

A melancholy thought of Deb passed through. Paige deserved someone better than me.

"You're thinking of her." Paige had a way of reading my mind.

Our waitress returned and she set a white wine in front of Paige and a glass of Scotch in front of me.

"Don't think of denying it." Paige gave me a soft, knowing smile. "You were thinking of Deb."

"I was, but it's nothing." I took a sip of the Scotch and let it coat my mouth before swallowing.

"Your divorce is final this month, isn't it?" She asked the question, but her eyes revealed she knew the answer.

She took a draw on her wine, breaking eye contact. I followed the direction of her gaze to a couple who sat so close to each other it was probably best they call it a night, head upstairs and finish the deal.

"Hard to believe that Fields is dead." I desperately needed a change of subject.

She closed her eyes briefly.

I continued. "You know when Jack and I spoke to Fields, he told us he didn't drink. That was obviously a lie."

"Not necessarily. He was grieving and heartbroken." She leaned on the table, her arms folded, one hand pinched around the stem of her wine glass. "People act differently under those circumstances."

I don't know why I was avoiding the one topic of conversation she wanted to have. Maybe it was because I knew giving in to the situation, one I wasn't able to pursue, hurt too much. It was like losing Deb all over again. It was best that I not let myself get involved. Or was it too late?

Soft curls of red hair framed Paige's face. Her green eyes seemed dull and I witnessed the pain in them, but what was I supposed to do about it? Risk my career? Risk hers? I couldn't be responsible for that.

My mind went to the case—safe ground. Fields' prints didn't match the partial on the silver tape pulled from Ellis and there was no missing chrome from his truck's hitch. Our killer was still in the wind.

"Seems we won't be headed home anytime soon." The words came out and I assessed their value—mindless chatter. We were better than that, weren't we?

She took another draw on her wine without responding.

I hated seeing her this way. "You're sad because it's almost Christmas and you're here?"

"What makes you say that?"

"The way you're being."

"And how is that?"

"You seem upset. I know you love Christmas."

"There are other things I love besides Christmas." She took a sip of wine.

"Listen," I took a deep breath, "I know how you feel about me."

"Ha. You know how I feel? About you?" She sank back into the booth. "I don't even know why I bother trying to hold on, Brandon.

What's the point? Tell me, would you?"

I took a gulp of the Scotch. It burned all the way down, but I was too stubborn to show any indication of it.

"You send me mixed signals. First, you push me away, then you pull me in, and the cycle repeats over and over again." She drew circles in the air, then dropped her hand. "Do you love me?"

Her question punched me in the gut. Fuck, yes, I loved her! Were we meant to be together? I didn't believe in that crap right now.

I took another sip.

"I'm tired of hanging around waiting for you to see if something better is coming along, Brandon. I'm letting you go." Tears welled in her eyes as she stood up. "I have to." She swigged back the rest of her wine and tossed a ten dollar bill on the table and walked away.

I let her go.

CHAPTER 34

THE NEWS WAS ALL OVER THE PLACE. Kent Fields, a renowned Pulitzer-winning author, was dead. He died on scene when his car wrapped around the base of a tree. The Advocate heard the recap as he channel flipped, hoping that this was some sort of cruel joke.

He had everything figured out and it wasn't supposed to happen like this. Now who was going to take the fall? It certainly wasn't going to be him. Not after all the hard work and planning he put into this. He had to choose his next target very carefully.

Plans had to be changed, but that was life. He still had people to make pay. Just like a detour can occur on a long road trip, that was all this equated to. He would still reach his destination. The world would benefit from a cleaner and more just society.

He brought up the Internet and searched for his next victim. It seemed like his initial choice was granted a stay of life—for now. He'd move on and pick someone closer to home, and it would most certainly get the FBI's attention.

But was that what he wanted?

He told himself many times he wasn't a killer, even though the dead bodies contradicted that belief. He could justify his actions. These men deserved to die for what they had done. Even the Good Book believes in retribution, a compensating for sins.

He wasn't God's means of meting out justice. He wasn't that disillusioned, but he had a higher purpose. He wouldn't be stopped unless he wanted to. The best course of action would be to lie low until the FBI disappeared—the man hours and budget would eventually supersede the need to find a killer.

But there was a burning inside of him that couldn't be dampened. A compulsion that drove him forward. His hands shook when he stumbled upon the perfect person.

He smirked.

Yes, he would arrive. This was just the scenic route.

THE ADVOCATE HATED BEING THIS UNPREPARED, but he wasn't left with a choice. When he spotted his next target, he had a feeling it would be easier than he thought.

The Offender's gait tipped left to right as if he were a piece of fabric blowing in the breeze. He lost his footing on the step along the front walkway and came down hard, knee to concrete—his left one taking the brunt of it.

"Son of a bitch!"

His yell pierced the night air, but no one seemed to pay him attention. No lights turned on in the neighboring houses.

The Advocate took it as a sign to move. The superstitious part of him saw it as a positive omen that he was where he was supposed to be. He got out of the car and made it all the way to the man without being noticed.

"Here, would you like help?" He offered him a hand to stand up, but the recognized gesture of goodwill was only to ensure that the man would go quietly.

The Offender straightened out, a stupid grin on his face, and slurred, "Thanks, man."

It was time to act. The Advocate pulled the gun from his coat.

The ridiculous expression on the man's face morphed into fear. He batted his hands in the air. "Get away—"

"Be quiet. You come with me, nice and slow and I won't shoot you." He preferred he followed his advice. He'd rather him suffer long, slow, and painfully as he had inflicted on one of the defenseless.

"Who are you?" Even standing back up, he leaned side to side. His breath stank of cheap whiskey.

"That doesn't matter. See that car over there? The one behind me?"

The drunk squinted. His eyes were glazed over like two beady marbles. "Why does it matter?"

God, he had no toleration for drunks. He pressed the gun to the man's gut. "You're going to walk there like we're friends."

"Hey, I've seen you before."

I highly doubt it.

"Move it." He gestured with a nudge of the gun.

The Offender held up his hands and toppled forward.

Maybe he had underestimated the simplicity of this abduction. But patience. The man would pay for what he did, and it would be executed flawlessly. He would see to that.

He put him in the small room where Lyons had decided to hang himself rather than endure more physical pain and discomfort. He was weak, giving up on life. No doubt he realized that he was a miserable being who didn't deserve the breath of life.

Either way it was of no consequence. The sacrifice of atonement had been made—adhering to Biblical logic—a life for a life.

He had the latest Offender constrained to a chair. Restraints were on his arms, his ankles, and for good measure, a clasp was around his neck. The latter hardly fit around him and had his eyes bulging and bloodshot—red lines spread out like vines. Still, there would be no mercy.

Above him was a jug of hydrofluoric acid. He had added water to ensure that he'd have longer to toy with the man, to make him realize the error in his ways.

"Do you know why you're here?" he asked.

His captive looked at him with eyes like blank coals.

"You are going to get back what you deserve. See above you?" He paused as if the man were able to accept the invitation. "Well, I guess you can't. So I will tell you. Better yet, I will show you."

He snapped on gloves.

"Please, no, don't do this."

The Advocate moved to the container and punctured the base of it with a fine-tipped awl.

Even with protection, he hurried to get his hand out of the way, but he was too slow. A few drops burned through to flesh.

The cry coming from his throat mingled with the curdling screams of his captive.

Suddenly any pain he experienced paled to insignificance. "You are only getting back what you deserve." He ripped off his gloves and left the room. He would leave the jug to run dry and his captive to receive the rewards of his actions.

CHAPTER 35

THE CASE SEEMED TO BE getting nowhere fast. The lab was still working on tying the chrome paint from the hitch to a truck brand. We didn't have any other hot suspects at the moment.

We were at the field office deciding our next course of action.

"We still haven't spoken to Karl Ball's wife. He's the missing man from two thousand ten," Paige said.

She hadn't looked at me all morning, and after a night of tossing and turning myself, I don't think I blamed her. She was right, but things were what they were.

"We've done a lot of talking to family members." Jack's eyes showed he was in thought. "All right, we know both Ellis and Lyons were gamblers. Could our unsub be a man they both owed money to?"

"Good luck finding that person though, especially if they owed someone under the table," Zachery said.

"Hmm."

"What about casinos in the area? Did they owe them?" I asked. Everyone but Paige had their attention on me.

"Not sure. We should ask Nadia to look into that aspect."

"We need to figure out where their lives could have intersected."

Paige's phone chimed and I recognized it as being an email notification. She pulled out her cell and pushed some buttons. "Well, I got my answer from Nadia on prior politicians. You're not going to believe who is on the list. Detective Hogan's father was mayor for one term, twenty-six years ago."

"You're thinking maybe he was involved with Lyons getting

off?" Zachery asked.

"What is the point of going down this path? I don't understand."

If a glare could freeze Tahiti…

Paige's jaw tightened and her mouth fell into a straight line. "It's called being thorough."

"All right, but we're not suspecting that he's responsible for the killings are we? I mean why help get a man off and then carry out his own justice?" I answered my own question. The guy we were after had an ego. He was selective. "Never mind."

"On top of it, our killer would know the charges are essentially a slap on the hand." Paige didn't acknowledge my presence when she continued. "It would also explain something else. Detective Hogan said he didn't hate people, just the feds. Hogan Senior spent some time with the Bureau."

"Maybe it's time to find out why he hated his father so much. He might know more than he's telling us," Zachery reasoned.

PAIGE MANAGED TO CONVINCE JACK it would be best if she approached Detective Hogan alone. She worked it from the standpoint that she could use her female charm and work it in their favor. He waved her off to take care of it.

The plea hadn't stemmed from honest intentions though. She needed to get away from Brandon. How could he be so obtuse? It hurt just being around him. His moods ran polar opposite and it would have her questioning his mental stability if she didn't know better.

But how could he go from kissing her to the cool indifference he had demonstrated in the bar? The way he tried to divert the conversation to Christmas and to the case. There was only one subject they needed to discuss and that was their relationship. She hated being toyed with and she didn't understand why, when it came to him, she let it happen repeatedly.

She pulled into the Starbucks lot and picked out the department-issued sedan immediately. There was a spot open beside it and she parked there.

She found Detective Hogan sitting at a corner table, cradling a festive paper cup bearing the name of the chain. She slipped in across from him.

He noticed her empty hands. "Not having anything?"

"Not really in the mood." She took her coat off and put it on the back of the chair.

He studied her. "I know I told you the getting-to-know-me part of the day was to be during personal time…are you going for that now?" He smiled, and a shot of derision for all men bolted through Paige's system.

"Actually, I wanted to tell you that I know why you hate the feds."

He raised his cup and jutted it toward her. "I'm actually surprised it took you this long."

"Let's just say that it was on my to-do list, but not at the very top." She grinned at him, the way she had perfected to lure men closer.

"Oh. *Touché.*"

"Tell me about your father."

"You wanting the abbreviated version? Because if you want the long story, I suggest you get some caffeine in you."

She laughed. "I've drunk enough lately to power the city. Surprised I even got any sleep last night." The truth was she hadn't slept, but it wasn't the result of any stimulant. How could Brandon just let her walk away? She shook the thought, focusing back on Hogan. "How did he hurt you?"

Hogan laughed this time. "What? My father? You're trying to get me to open up by appealing to my emotions? I'm a man, I don't work that way. I do like your shirt though."

She didn't even glance down. It was a button-up number, in a shade of green that suited her, and she had purposely left the top three buttons undone to hint at the cleavage beneath the fabric. She took the compliment—she was on the right track. Most men's minds worked the same way.

"All right, I'll get to the point," she said.

"That would be wonderful." He cradled his cup with both hands.

He was retreating from the conversation. It was a surefire sign when someone put things in front of their chest or held something with two hands when one would do.

"I didn't look into your past to get close to you."

He placed one hand over his heart but was quick to return it to the cup.

She smirked. "Your father's name only came up in a search I had done."

He leaned forward. "Don't tell me you think he's involved with the killings somehow."

She proceeded without responding to his concern. "A victim's wife told me that her husband had gotten off because he knew someone who knew someone."

"Wow, and that *someone* led back to my father?"

"It did. I had our girl research those in any position of power at the time the charges were laid, and there was your last name."

"Nice to know you were thinking of me." His eyes sparkled.

He was obviously doing his best to pour on what charm he could muster. But after what Brandon had done to her last night, it would take a lot more than flirtatious eyes and smiles to dampen the hatred she felt for the male sex.

"Your father served for a brief stint with the Bureau, but that's probably not the real reason you hate us."

"*Curious and curiouser.*" He settled back in his chair and put both hands on his cup.

"Your father did some things you weren't proud of when he was a mayor." She was fishing and hoped he didn't realize.

"Hmm, well, he changed after being with the FBI, so I pin the blame there."

"All fine and good, but we believe that maybe your father got Simpson off from the charges against him for animal abuse."

He scoffed. "You've got to be fucking kidding me." He raised eyes to the ceiling, and then down to meet Paige's. "My father was not in the picture when I was young. He didn't care about me. He cared about solving cases and then when that came to an end, he cared about votes. I highly doubt he knew a man like Simpson, let alone got close to him."

Paige let the silence build for about thirty seconds. "Do you think he would have—"

"Gotten a man off from abuse charges? Absolutely not." He let go of his cup. "Are we done here?"

Paige nodded and Hogan got up and left.

Maybe she would sit there for a while and let her thoughts gel. She believed Hogan, but until they had their killer in custody, she had to tuck the facts of this meeting away in case they were needed.

Her cell rang. "Special Agent Dawson."

"Paige?"

"What is it, Brandon?" She wasn't in the mood to hear an apology and she certainly wasn't open to being manipulated.

"There's another one."

"Another one? A victim?"

"Missing. Get back to the office."

"I'll be right there." She grabbed her coat and hung up, disappointed that he hadn't called to fight for her in spite of her anger toward him.

Chapter 36

Detectives McClellan and Hogan were in the briefing room at the field office, updating us on the latest missing person case.

Hogan arrived a moment ago, appearing agitated. Seeing as Paige hadn't gotten in, I assumed their meeting hadn't gone well.

McClellan ensured he had our attention. "The man went missing only yesterday morning but given his history and the circumstances, the report was generated anyhow."

"Elaborate," Jack said.

"His name is Warren Howell. He was reported by his common-law wife, Melissa, when he didn't come home last night. Apparently, the guy has a habit of heavy drinking and staying out late with the guys, so it wasn't until this morning that she suspected something was wrong."

"And he abused a dog?" Jack said.

"Yes, but his case doesn't go back twenty-six years. It goes back six months."

"Six months," Zachery reiterated.

I remembered Detective Hogan's skeptical nature from a couple of days ago. Our eyes connected. "Let me guess, you think it's a serial now."

He was about to respond, his open mouth clamped shut—Paige's timing was impeccable as she walked into the room and dropped her coat on the table.

"We just started." Zachery brought her up to speed.

Paige disregarded him and said, "I heard you say the charges on the latest vic were just laid six months ago? Our unsub is changing his game."

"But that isn't the strangest part," McClellan said. "Our guy did show up at home, but then disappeared between his car and the front door."

"Come again?" I said.

"Well, his wife was in bed and saw the lights from his car shine in the window. She even heard him lock the car doors—the irritating honk they do these days. She said she drifted off to sleep after that, but when she woke up this morning his vehicle was there, but he was nowhere to be found. That's when she called us."

"So he was taken from his property?" I asked.

"Seems like it. We conducted a search of their backyard. We assume that he came home drunk."

"What about surrounding houses? It wouldn't be uncommon for someone in that condition to wander." I remembered my grandmother telling me about a drunk neighbor man who had let himself in and slept on her couch. It was probably another reason—besides the fact I knew what people were capable of—that I made certain to lock my doors all the time.

McClellan shook his head. "No sign of him at all. That's why we're here."

I realized that I was the only one from our team talking and surveyed everyone in the room.

Hogan's arms were crossed, his jaw tight, his eyes focused. Paige's arms were tight to her sides and her hands were in her pockets. They seemed to be avoiding each other. Jack and Zachery were standing back observing.

"Fields is dead. If the killer was trying to pin the murders on someone—specifically Fields—he's out of luck there. Why not just cool off for a bit? Wait for us to go away?" I asked.

"He's getting cocky at this point. He doesn't think we can stop him. Maybe he's still disillusioned that he can cast blame elsewhere," Zachery reasoned.

"Evidence pointed to Bowen. Then to Fields," I ruminated. "What do these men hold in common with our killer? Their lines of work were entirely different. It must go back further than that."

Jack pointed the end of an unlit cigarette toward me. "That is something worth looking into."

I dialed Nadia and had her pry further into their backgrounds.

"We can't be too late for Howell. Do you understand?" Jack scanned his team. With his gaze came the warning that we were to focus, or we might as well pack up and head home. He'd be willing to send us there.

I finished with Nadia and put the phone back in my pocket. "Who wrote the article on Howell?" I asked Detective McClellan, who seemed to have shrunk back against the wall. For a law enforcement officer, he didn't fare well under Jack's permeating glare.

"Brent Turner. He's new and still wet behind the ears." He glanced at Jack. "I had that information pulled right away."

"We should go speak with him," I said.

Paige's eyes were cold. "You're really setting your sights on another reporter?"

"I think it's worth checking him out. I'm being thorough."

With her earlier words to me, served back to her, she glared at me and crossed her arms.

"We mentioned our killer is probably hiding in plain sight. How perfect. One reporter frames another."

"Pending could have a point, Boss. Turner might figure that we'd never suspect him. Two reporters in a row?"

"But what's his motivation?" Paige asked. "Would Turner even know Fields?"

I laughed. "Everyone in publishing would know Fields."

"Brandon."

Usually, I loved the sound of my name coming off Paige's lips, but right now my emotional response was to be defensive. Somehow, I managed to keep my mouth shut.

"You know what I mean, don't you?" Her tone was condescending. "What would make this personal to Turner? Why frame Fields? What was his trigger?"

"Paige is right. We've got to find out their history and see if it intersects," Jack said.

There was a hint of a smirk on Paige's lips as she pulled out her cell phone and dialed Nadia. Seconds later, she said, "I've got you on speaker. It's the team and two detectives from Denver PD—McClellan and Hogan."

"What's up? Brandon just called."

Paige carried on like she didn't even care about Nadia's response. "This is Nadia at headquarters. She's our go-to girl for information," Paige explained to the detectives. "Nadia, there's been another abduction. We need you to see if you can find anything that would connect Brent Turner with Kent Fields, besides the newspaper."

"Brandon just asked me to delve into Bowen and Fields to see how their lives intersected—beyond the obvious thing with them being stepbrothers."

Paige's cheeks blushed. "Maybe this is something you could do quickly for us?"

"Hang on a sec. It's possible something might strike right away. It didn't with the other two." Clicking of keys came over the speaker. "Oh."

The line went silent.

"Nadia?"

"Yeah, they have a connection all right. Turner was up for a prestigious writing award, but Fields walked away with it."

"There's our motivation." Paige regarded everyone in the room, her eyes resting on me a moment longer than the others, basking in the gloating. She turned her attention back to Nadia. "What about Turner's background?"

"Well, he's fairly young, right. Only twenty-seven. For him to even be up for that award is something."

"What about a criminal record?"

"No. Nothing. Very clean. Even a quick credit check came back spotless."

"That's interesting. No student loans?" I asked.

"One sec…No, but I do show that he went to Stanford University."

"No debt and he went there? He must have money." I still owed for my schooling.

More keys clicked. "He was favored with a fully paid scholarship."

McClellan let out a whistle.

"Where did Fields go?"

Paige shot me a derisive glare as if I were monopolizing the conversation. Last I knew we were a team. How many times had I been lectured by Jack that we were to work together? I dismissed her by raising my brows.

"Same. Stanford."

"And Bowen?"

"Stanford. Wait a minute. It doesn't appear that he made it that long. He dropped out in the middle of his first year."

"Well, you don't have to pry further into their backgrounds. We have our answer. Our unsub went to Stanford."

Paige didn't give up ground. "You're forgetting the age difference, Brandon. There are thirty years between them and Turner. They wouldn't have crossed paths there."

"Are you certain? A lot of times, successful people will return to their university and give lectures to the students—alumni and all that. They could have met on one of those occasions." I was feeling smug.

"And from one meeting Turner decided that he was going to frame the guy for murder some day?" Red saturated Paige's cheeks.

"You are forgetting the coveted award."

Her tongue flicked out between her lips and had me thinking of an animal about to pounce on its prey, but the intention wasn't carnal, it was sheer destruction.

"Actually," Nadia began, "Fields did return to give a lecture. It lines up with when Turner would have been a student."

It took all my willpower not to flash Paige an I-told-you-so smirk.

"All right, that's good for now, Nadia," Jack said with a warning glare at Paige and me.

"One more thing," Nadia began, "the warrant came through for the shelter employees. I'll send it over."

The line went dead, and Paige swooped her phone into a pocket.

McClellan walked closer to the table where we were sitting. "You guys think that maybe this young reporter was framing Fields all along?"

"We'll find out. We'll go pay him a visit. And, you guys," Jack referred to Paige and Zachery, "will deliver the warrant and collect our information from the shelter. Zach, we've got to hurry on this."

"I got it."

It was advantageous having a genius on the team who could read at the speed of light, and it didn't hurt that he retained all of it afterward either.

Chapter 37

THE PAPER'S CHIEF EDITOR WAS Saul Larson. He presented himself with large smiles and open eyes, but I suspected he was a sly man. There was something that lurked beneath the surface. Although, I suppose in this business he'd need to be a bit ruthless. He wore black-framed glasses that were round and wide.

Jack and I were in his office.

"You can speak with Brent as soon as he gets back, but I'm not sure when that will be. I've got him out following a lead." Larson leaned back in his plush office chair. The top of his desk was covered in papers, fanned in every possible direction, some even strewn over his keyboard.

"Does he not have a cell phone?" Jack asked.

"He does, but I don't like to bother my people when they're out getting news. It can hurt the creative flow doing something like that."

"You get on the phone or we'll wonder if you are trying to cover for him."

Larson kept his attention on Jack. "Why are you after Brent anyhow? The kid's pretty much fresh out of school. He gets local news."

"That's exactly why we want to see him."

"Listen, if you want to get the word out about something, tell it to me. I'll make sure it gets assigned to our best. I might even write it myself." He snapped forward. His left hand held a pen, which I suspected was worth a lot of money. It wasn't a cheap ballpoint. He tapped the end of it in his other hand.

"Nice pen," I said. Being an editor must pay well.

"I'll stay true to the facts. I won't let anything get out that you don't want to be heard. I already know that you're in town investigating the murders of Darren Simpson and Clyde Ellis." He smiled again, a more cocky display than any previous ones. "We've covered the stories. Let us—let me—take the story from the inside out. I can focus on the FBI, on you guys, what you're doing with the investigation. It would be the breaking-news headline the paper needs."

Neither Jack nor I said anything.

Larson held up his pen and addressed me. "I paid over two hundred for it."

And just when I didn't even think he heard my comment about the pen.

"That's a lot for something to write with."

"Yes, but once you have one you'll never go back. Here, do you want to hold it?" He extended it me, and I was about to reach for it when Jack glared at me.

"We're not here to give you a story. We do, however, need to speak with Brent Turner."

"Like I told you, he's out in the field. I would think he'd be back soon." Larson's eyes lit. "Is he a suspect?"

"Brent Turner has information we believe will prove useful."

"You think he could help you find the killer?"

I could hear it in Larson's tone of voice. He wasn't quite sure whether he should be taking Jack's claim at its straight value or question the words. Still, he gathered papers aside to reach the phone.

"Call on speaker," Jack said.

Larson shot Jack a snide glare, but it melted into another quirky smile.

By the third ring, a winded Brent Turner picked up.

"I need you to come down to the office right away."

"I'm working, Saul."

"Good as that is, I have two feds here to see you."

"Feds? Why are they—"

"Just get down here. Now."

"Sure." Turner sounded irritated and then disconnected the call.

"Well, if you want coffee or anything," Larson offered.

"We'll be fine."

ABOUT THIRTY MINUTES LATER, Brent Turner shadowed the doorway of Larson's office both loaded down and wearing drenched boots. It was good timing too. I sensed if Jack and I had to talk with Larson much longer, Jack would have said something he really shouldn't have. His need for a cigarette was getting desperate and had him reaching for his pocket at least five times in the last ten minutes.

I was about to stand up, but Brent Turner made it over to us before I could. He adjusted the strap of his laptop bag on his shoulder.

His hair was blond, and his eyes beamed with a zest for life. He was trim and it was apparent, despite the rushed lifestyle of a reporter, he made time for an exercise regimen.

Turner dropped into a chair and put his bag on the floor at his feet. I noticed that even though it was off his shoulder, he'd ensured that it was not out of reach. He let it lean against his leg as if by maintaining contact with it he would also maintain control.

He rubbed his hands on his thighs and looked past me to Jack. "I'm not sure why you want to talk to me." He gave a quick glance at his boss, which seemed to silently plead his innocence of any wrongdoing.

Larson directed him back to Jack with a pointed finger.

"You've heard of the murdered men? Darren Simpson and Clyde Ellis?"

"Of course. We covered their stories."

I sensed he was going to elaborate but was silenced by Jack's eye contact.

"There's another missing man."

Turner didn't glance at his boss as Larson kept his focus locked on the reporter's profile. There was something that wasn't being communicated, and I had the feeling I knew what it was.

"We apologize that we pulled you from a story." I opted for

getting on his good side. I received another glower from Jack for my trouble.

"Oh. Don't worry about it. I think I got everything I needed." His eyes shifted to Larson now.

"What's it about?" I drew his attention back to me with the question. I had a hunch the story he was chasing was at the heart of this investigation.

"Well, it's best not to say. Hope you understand." Turner plastered on a smile, one I'm sure he could use to get himself past police lines if need be, but his charm wasn't going to work on me.

"Is the story about Warren Howell?" I asked.

Jack's eyebrows shot up and the hand that had been over his shirt pocket lowered.

Turner's eyes shifted between the three of us as if not wanting to settle on any of us. Eventually, he focused on his boss.

Larson leaned forward and clasped his hands on the desk. "For good reason, we keep our sources and stories close to the vest until they go public. It's part of doing business."

Jack stood and slapped photographs on Larson's desk. They were pictures of the dogs abused by Simpson and Ellis.

"Part of doing business? What about this one?"

He dropped the photograph of Howell's Boxer. "He never survived." He put the picture of Howell on the desk. "Now this man is missing," a pointed finger went level with Turner's nose, "and you wrote the original article on the abuse charges."

Panic swept over Turner's features. When he spoke his voice was low and gravelly. "I don't know anything about his disappearance."

Jack narrowed his eyes on Turner. "Are you sure about that?" He held the eye contact for a few seconds. Turner broke it to glance at his boss.

"Did you see this?" Jack flicked the picture of Howell's injured dog from Larson's desk and shoved it in Turner's face.

Turner covered his mouth and his cheeks swelled. He took time to compose himself and then turned to Larson. "Can I tell them?"

CHAPTER 38

PAIGE AND ZACHERY WENT INTO the animal shelter and were greeted by Alisha holding onto the cat again.

"You're back?" Alisha regarded Paige's hand. "The warrant?"

"You would be correct." Paige gave it to her. Although happy the legality had finally come together, she couldn't help but wonder why some were issued so much faster than others. "Would Kim Delaney be here?"

"Absolutely. I will get her for you. Actually, why don't you just follow me back?" Clutching the piece of paper, Alisha ran her hand down the cat's back, loose hairs flying out in its wake.

Kim Delaney was at her desk, tapping away on the keyboard. She stopped typing but didn't seem as pleased to see them as Alisha had been. "Agents?"

"They have a warrant, Kim." Alisha handed the paperwork over and stepped back.

Delaney examined it and dropped it on her desk. "Well, then. It seems I can help you out. If you want to have a seat while you wait, this will take a while."

Alisha slipped out of the room.

"We understand it will, but if you could answer a few quick questions first," Zach said.

"Sure." The single word was drawn out.

"Kent Fields. He was a large donor but did he ever get hands-on involved?"

"I don't think so. He was too busy with his publishing career. Otherwise, I think he would have. Kent Fields—what a tragedy there."

News spread fast, and bad news had wings.

"It was. We had asked you before about any volunteers who would get really upset over animal abuse cases."

Delaney nodded.

"We got the impression you had some names."

"There are so many of them. Honestly, even I get worked up. To witness what people—we'll say *people* in quotations—do, it breaks my heart. They are more animal than the animals."

"You had told us about how the charges work last time we were here. There would be a lot of anger when this is being executed I would assume," Paige said.

"Absolutely. It's at the core of mankind—at least I believe so—to find justice. We know that we're only the first step in getting this for those animals. The rest is out of our hands."

"Did you ever have anyone become physically violent at one of these scenes, or afterward?"

Delaney gave it a few seconds, deep in thought. "I do remember this guy from years ago. Darn, what was his name? He actually put his hands on the dog owner's neck. A few of us had to pull him off."

"And you don't remember his name?" Zach asked.

"No, sorry. It should be written up in a file somewhere. I'm not sure. You'll be getting everything I have."

"You mentioned most of you get angry. Anyone else stand out to you?"

"There is someone." Her eyes flickered as if she hesitated to share the name. "He would see what these people did and say that there's one thing that could move him to murder. The thing is, he didn't strike me as a violent person, but the way he would get this twitch in his cheek when he spoke about it."

"About *it*?"

Delaney leveled eyes with Zach. "He said he'd have no problem repaying these people in kind for their treatment of these animals. Said that they deserved it for what they had done."

"You mentioned he'd speak about it *after* seeing what they had done. Was he a volunteer?"

"No. He was a reporter. Brent Turner."

Chapter 39

There were several seconds of silence that followed Turner's question to Larson about whether he should give us any details. I had an inkling, and I was certain Jack did as well.

"Should you tell us *what*?" Jack asked, nailing in the fact that we needed answers now.

"Brent just came from Howell's place," Larson said. The ever-present grin had finally subsided. "We're just doing our jobs."

"Just doing your jobs? Hmm."

"Listen it's not like it's illegal to talk to people. You can't stop us…free speech and all."

"Why did you go?" Jack asked Turner.

"I don't understand what you mean."

"You're the one who covered the story originally when Howell was charged. I'm sure his wife wasn't too happy to see you."

Turner's mouth gaped open. No words came out.

"How did she react to seeing you there?"

Larson held both hands, palms out, motioning for Turner to lay it all out there for us.

"We hear everything over the police scanners. We knew that Howell was missing. We also know about his past. Obviously." Turner's eyes went between Jack and me. "It was decided since I had history there, I would cover the piece. I actually fought for it."

Regret was evident on both Turner's and Larson's faces.

"I'd like to know why you fought for it," Jack said.

"Really? It's big news. Two men have been killed and another one goes—"

"Jump ahead to the real reason."

Turner pressed his hands on his thighs, and then one of them reached down and brushed the top of his laptop bag. Seemingly content it was still there, he angled his head to the left and continued. "It was my opportunity for a breakout story."

"It's only about the ratings?"

Jack didn't seem convinced, and I held my suspicions as well. Here we'd had a man who had easy access to all animal abuse cases the paper had covered and a direct connection with Howell. Now he was eager to talk to the man's wife? Was it just out of hunger for front-page placement, or was it to get close and find out how the investigation was being handled? A means of prodding the woman into saying things the police had asked her about?

"I can see you doubt me, both of you, but that's all it was, I swear."

"So you didn't go there to get close to the investigation?"

"Yeah, but not in the way you're implying."

"Hmm."

"No, seriously." He held up his hands. "I covered this man's case. I know you know that. But I just felt the story needed to be told by me. No one else. I was there when that dog was brought into the shelter. Well, I wasn't there, I saw it anyway. It was barely alive and then it was pronounced." Turner's voice held grief and anger.

"Sounds like you were quite mad about it."

"Of course I was. Have you ever seen an abused animal...after?"

His question put me back in time, to when Deb was home. It was impossible for her to watch those television commercials that depicted neglected or injured animals. In contrast, I couldn't imagine it having the same effect on Jack. Turner was trying to elicit empathy from the wrong man.

"I've seen worse," was Jack's answer.

His statement was enough to cloak the room in silence. I figured he referred to both his job with the FBI and his military service.

His phone vibrated and he answered.

His eyes shifted from Larson, and then settled on Turner. "We're with him right now."

Turner swallowed roughly and audibly. He reached for the bag at his feet and picked it up. He was good at reading body language and when Jack told him he'd be coming with us, he was calmer than Larson, who yelled out behind us.

"I'll get you a lawyer. Don't say anything."

I had a feeling the only thing Larson was actually concerned about was the reputation of his paper, not Turner's future.

CHAPTER 40

BRENT TURNER'S CONFIDENT DEMEANOR HAD been replaced by panic. His cheeks were flushed and his eyes jabbed about the room. I imagined he was thinking about his future and how it was a bleak projection.

The lawyer that Larson had promised still hadn't shown up, and Turner, who must have been more eager to get things moving along, waived away his right.

Jack sat across from him in the interrogation room. I stood behind him, against the wall.

Jack laid out a bunch of pictures in front of Turner, one by one, putting them on the table with dramatic flair.

First, the one of Simpson with his dog, followed by his body in the alley.

Second, Ellis and his dog, then his mangled body.

Third, Howell and his dog.

"It looks like we might be missing a picture," Jack said.

Turner refused to glance at the photos.

Jack raised his voice. "You killed these men."

"I didn't. I swear to you."

"You were furious when animals were abused."

"Who told—yes, I did. I do. It's wrong on so many levels."

"Yet you reported on these cases. You put yourself around them."

"I didn't have much of a choice."

"Hmm."

"These men," Jack pressed a finger, first to the photo of Simpson, and then Ellis, "these were old cases, dating back twenty-six years ago."

"Yeah, I was just a baby."

To hear him put it like that made me realize how young I was in the scheme of things myself. Turner and I were only two years apart.

"Doesn't matter. They were killed in the last couple of weeks." Jack put down photographs of Karl Ball and Dean Garner.

"Who are they?"

Jack smiled. It was predatory. "You sure you don't know who they are?"

"Should I?"

"They went missing back in two thousand nine and ten."

"Well, I don't even know who they are."

"But you know who this is?" Jack put a professional photograph of Kent Fields on the top of the rest.

Turner glanced down only for a split second. "Of course I do."

"What did you think of Mr. Fields?" Jack leaned back in his chair.

"I'm not sure what you're getting at."

"Just that. You knew him."

"I knew *of* him."

"Hmm."

Turner looked past Jack to me. "I don't understand. Obviously you know more than I do."

"You were up for the same award, against a Pulitzer-winning journalist. It must have been quite an ego boost."

Turner gave a slight nod as if by doing so it was a confession of wrongdoing somehow.

"But you didn't win, did you? He claimed the award at the very end. Crushing your dreams."

"I moved on."

"But that wasn't the first time you ran into Kent Fields, was it?"

Turner rubbed his hands together on the table. "I'm not sure what you're getting at."

"Let me refresh your memory. You both went to the same university."

Turner blurted out a laugh. "Years apart."

Jack's face remained stoic. "But he came back to deliver a lecture, didn't he? One you were in attendance for."

"How do you know all this, and what are you implying? Please just tell me." Turner addressed his words to me.

Jack turned toward me as if tagging me to take over.

I pushed off the wall. "We believe that you framed Kent Fields for the murders of Simpson and Ellis. When things got messed up, meaning he died, wrapping his car around a tree, you had to change your victim pool." I had elaborated on Fields' cause of death to prompt a reaction. Turner provided none.

"Victim pool? Framing Fields? No, no way. You're saying I'm the killer?" Turner retched into his mouth and swallowed it back down. "You can't prove any of this."

"Here's the wonderful part. We can hold you for at least forty-eight hours without needing to charge you. That will give us plenty of time to ensure we have all the evidence we need."

"No. Please. I'll tell you anything you need to know, but I didn't kill those people." Turner ran a hand through his hair, his eyes were moist with tears. Fear was embedded there.

I'm sure he was rethinking his decision to waive his right to a lawyer.

"Listen, those stories? It wasn't my idea. It's where the new guy starts out."

"You seem to bring a lot of passion to the table though. The manager at the shelter said you would be willing to murder an animal abuser. She said, and I quote, that you would have 'no problem repaying these people in kind for their treatment of these animals.'"

Turner held up a hand and took a deep breath. "What she said, it's true. I did say that, but I didn't act on it."

"We've got two bodies and three missing people. Somebody acted on it," Jack said.

"Yeah, *somebody*, not me. Like I said, I'd rather be reporting other kinds of stories. You mentioned people went missing in two thousand nine and ten? I was still living in California."

"You told us not long ago that you fought to have this story about Howell."

"About him going missing, not about him abusing the dog. Local news, animal abuse, they're not going to advance my career. I don't have a choice about what I write. I'm told what to write." He probed my eyes and then Jack's. "I didn't kill anyone."

"You said you are assigned these stories. By whom?"

I glanced at Jack. He beat me to the question.

A knock came on the door, and Jack's glare had me jumping to answer.

Paige and Zachery were there. Both of them were winded.

CHAPTER 41

BRENT TURNER WAS LEFT IN the interrogation room while Paige and Zachery shared their findings.

"When we were at the shelter executing the warrant, we spoke with the manager. She told us about a volunteer from years ago who got violent with an animal owner when they went to collect the abused animals. She said that he had his hands around the man's neck and it took a couple of them to pry them off." Paige paced around the table in the conference room. "She couldn't remember his name but said something may have been noted in the files. When we were working through the volunteer information, we found him. At first, his name didn't mean anything to us, but we had Nadia complete a full background check. Well, it's Saul Larson."

"That's the newspaper editor," I said.

"That's right."

"Turner was just telling us that he doesn't pick these animal abuse stories, they are assigned to him."

"And who else would know about all of these cases as well as the editor?" Zachery flashed a knowing smile.

"We had him in our reach and we took in the wrong guy."

"Hold on, Kid. We're not jumping right in this time. Tell us what Nadia found out on him."

Zachery went first. "Saul Larson went to university with Kent Fields and Craig Bowen. Fields and he were both up for the same job, but Fields beat him out."

"It seems everything that Larson went after, Fields actually took out from under him," Paige added.

"Could be motive for framing Fields. He went on to the big time while Larson is stuck behind an editor's desk with the local paper," I said.

"Big city, but, exactly." Paige slipped into a chair across from me. "But here is where it gets really interesting. We had Nadia search for any suspicious deaths that were around any location Larson lived."

"We found one," Zachery pitched in. "It's a neighborhood in Denver."

Paige continued. "We figured our killer is from the local area, striking close to his home. Anyway, what started off as a shot in the dark came back with a huge payoff."

"The man's name was Ken Bailey." Zachery wouldn't be defeated. He held a hand up to Paige and smiled. She returned it.

"I'm still listening." Jack was leaned across the table.

"It gets even better, Boss. This guy, Bailey, had a dog. Now, according to records he went missing twenty-six years ago."

"Hmm."

"He was found four years ago."

"He's alive?" I asked.

Paige carried on. "Dead. He was found in his own house."

Zachery's turn. "The current homeowners were doing renovations and taking down a wall. Bailey was encased inside. It's amazing no one smelled him when it first happened, but apparently, the house sat empty for a long time. It isn't in the best neighborhood so didn't get too much interest. By the time it was sold, he would have dried right out."

All I could think about was people had lived in that house with a dead body behind the wall and never even knew it.

"Any leads on the case?" Jack asked.

"None. It's cold."

"A cold case that just got a whole lot warmer. Get them to pull the evidence," Jack directed.

"Already have, and they are."

"You mentioned this Bailey guy had a dog?" I asked.

"Oh yeah, I almost forgot to say this. So the guy went missing, but so did the dog. The guy turns up dead, but what happened to the dog?"

"We've got to get more on this, and on Larson, before we move. I want unmarked cars assigned to watch his house for anything suspicious. Saul Larson used to work with his father doing drywall. He would have had no problem sealing the man up a wall," Zachery said.

"We still need more information. Was Bailey ever charged with animal abuse?"

"No, Boss, and that explains why his death didn't come up in our previous search." Paige stopped walking.

"What was this guy's cause of death?"

Zachery answered. "Conclusion was blunt force trauma. He was beaten to death. Glass, from a rum bottle, was embedded in his forehead. Investigators reviewed pictures taken when Bailey first went missing. There were broken bottles and blood trace. Everything was collected, along with DNA. Still, no match in the system."

"Not surprising. I think we've already established our guy hasn't gotten caught. Yet."

I figured Jack added the latter word in the hopes of instilling confidence into his team. But there were times in an investigation when I wondered how wide we had to cast the net to catch a killer.

Chapter 42

Paige and Zack were at the police station reviewing the evidence collected in regards to Ken Bailey. Jack and Brandon were paying a quick visit to Howell's common-law wife.

Ironically, Detective McClellan, who was just an officer back then, was part of the original missing persons investigation. The initial lead on the case had died of a heart attack years back. McClellan was called in when the body was discovered four years ago. That time around, the lead was his.

Paige was asking him questions while Zach did what he did best—speed read.

"They didn't bring in dogs when he first went missing?" Paige asked.

"There was no way of knowing the guy was in the wall." McClellan had offered an odd smile before it fell sullen. "It was my first real crime scene and I only got to see it from the outside. There wasn't even a body. But I knew it then, you know, just that gut feeling that tells you something is off. I didn't have the pull to do anything about it. You know what it's like when you're working up the ranks." A small shoulder shrug. "Maybe you don't. But I was one of a few officers who went canvassing to see if anyone had seen or heard anything. I mean, it was obvious there was some type of struggle. It was revealed the guy liked to play his music loud, late at night. He also had a bad gambling habit. We thought maybe a bookie, or someone else, made good on threats and got rid of him."

"A lot of times those types don't try to cover things up. The hit's made obvious."

"What I thought, but we tried."

"I find it interesting that this is the third person to have a gambling habit and I'm starting to wonder if it factors in." Paige considered if it meant anything at all. Nadia couldn't find anything to indicate that Saul Larson had gambling issues. It was quite possible that aspect was just a false commonality and that it really had no bearing on the outworking of the investigation.

"One more question, Detective. You were one of the canvassing officers the first time around. Do you remember anyone who stood out to you?"

"My memory's good but not quite that good. We're talking the better part of thirty years ago. If there was, though, it would be in my notes."

Zach looked up from other investigative reports. "You didn't note anyone. In fact, no one did."

"Sorry that I couldn't have been of more help. This is a strange case, though, that is for sure. Bailey mummifies in a wall for over twenty years and then is found."

"Did he have any next of kin?" Paige asked McClellan.

Zach answered. "His cousin, Gregory Ford. Both parents were dead at the time Bailey's body was found."

McClellan smiled and held his hands out toward Zach. "What he said."

"All right. Who reported him missing?" Paige asked.

"It's in the file, Paige." Zach smiled at her. "His work."

"His work reported him missing? No loved ones, spouse, live-in?"

"No, even I remember that," McClellan chimed in. "I remember thinking about how alone he was. I also remember promising myself that if I ever went missing I'd want someone I loved, not my employer, reporting it."

"That is sad, isn't it?" Paige had a chill run through her and she wrapped her arms around herself. "Bailey would have been twenty-nine. That's plenty of time to set up a home, make friends, fall in love."

"Not everyone believes in love." A gentle smile from McClellan.

"Well, if you need anything, just holler. I've got some paperwork I better get started on. I keep hoping it will just go away, but it never does."

"Thank you."

Paige's smile faded when McClellan left the room. She turned to Zach, her expression serious. "What connection would Saul Larson have to Bailey?"

Zach put down a crime scene photo he had been intently studying. "From what I see, besides sharing a neighborhood twenty-six years ago, there's no evidence Larson and Bailey crossed paths." He paused. "Wait a minute. Larson's dad owned a construction company by the name of Prestigious Home Contractors. Can't believe I didn't tie it together until now. Bailey's file shows he worked for Prestigious."

"We have our connection."

CHAPTER 43

I WONDERED WHY JACK HAD us visiting Howell's common-law wife. Things were lining up against the editor, Saul Larson, but Jack still wanted more to solidify our case against him. I couldn't help but think about Howell's condition though. Would we be there in time to save him? Jack, who would normally move on less, held back. Why give us a mini-speech about stopping another murder if he was going to put on the brakes?

"And why aren't we going after Larson? He's looking good for this." My words fell hollow inside the SUV. I stared at Jack's profile. As usual a lit cigarette was perched between his lips.

He pulled it down and exhaled, but he didn't answer my question.

I continued. "We know he shared a neighborhood with a murdered guy from twenty-six years ago, he worked with him, he assigned the local news stories about animal abusers."

"He assigns all news stories, Kid. That isn't a crime."

Jack pulled into Howell's driveway and my stomach tossed. This wasn't going to be an easy visit. This would be close on scale with providing notification of kin, and in some ways worse, we had no news.

Melissa Byrd opened the front door. She had light blond hair, brown eyes, and dark eyebrows. The contrast made her eyes pop. "Come in."

I passed a glance at Jack. We didn't have to show our credentials and this woman openly accepted us into her home.

Jack started the formal introduction and Melissa waved her hand.

"I know who you are, well, who you're with. I can tell by that fancy SUV and the way you're dressed. You're professionals, but you're certainly not with Denver PD."

I found her energy hard to accept. This woman's significant other was missing, possibly dead. She couldn't have been immune to the news propagating around her.

"We're sorry that your—"

"We need to ask you some questions about your husband," Jack interrupted me.

"He was my boyfriend, really. We just lived together. He is terrified of marriage. It probably has something to do with the mess he was involved with before me. She was a needy one. Talk about not having your life in balance." Melissa *tsked* as she moved throw pillows from the couches to clear a place for us to sit. "You have to make time to journal and meditate every day. That's how you find your inner calm and can truly shine."

I imagined that inside Jack was growling from this woman's upbeat nature. I admired his restraint.

"Do you know this man?" Jack extended a photograph of Saul Larson that we pulled from his DMV records.

I noticed how he disregarded everything she had said.

"Oh, absolutely." She pushed it back toward Jack. "He's a family friend."

This woman's positive projection didn't mingle well with her current situation. Her boyfriend had been charged with pouring acid on a dog, now he was missing, and there was a serial killer pulling from that victim pool.

Jack took a seat and ran his hands downs his thighs to straighten his pant legs. I sat beside him.

"How long was he a family friend?" Jack asked.

"Oh, I don't know. Years. Saul's a good man."

Like your boyfriend? I thought sarcastically.

"Why are you asking about him? He's all right, I hope."

It dawned on me, she hadn't asked us once about Howell. There was no concern about his well-being, whether we had found him if he was alive or dead.

"How long were you and Warren Howell together?" I asked.

"Seven years." A smile accompanied her words.

Seven years, but she was able to easily dismiss him from her life. There was only one way to broach the subject that concerned me, and that was directly.

"You don't seem very upset that your husband—boyfriend—is missing."

Melissa made a clucking sound with her tongue. "That's because I've been repeating my positive mantras ever since he left."

"He left?" Interesting terminology. She was in denial that it wasn't of his own choice.

"Yes, I think so now."

"Were you having problems in the relationship?"

"Absolutely not." Another smile.

"But you still believe he left you?"

She nodded. "But I believe he'll be back. We're meant to be together." Her smile and happy aura finally faded. "I'm sure you think he's a horrible man for doing what he did to that dog."

No response was necessary.

"That wasn't the real him. He was drunk…and high. He wasn't thinking."

He wasn't thinking? It took every part of me to keep grounded to the couch. "Did he abuse you?"

An awkward few seconds of silence. "It's not about me. Have you found him?"

"No," Jack answered her.

Her eyes snapped to him and she studied his face. "Do you think he's been murdered?"

While the smile had disappeared, there were odd emotions coming off her. I tagged it as denial.

"We believe he's been taken against his will." Jack bobbed his head toward the photo of Larson. "Tell us more about him."

"What is there to say? He's a good man. He's been a friend of mine for a long time, Warren's even longer. He introduced me to him. Doesn't hurt having a big shot as a friend." The smiles were back.

What she said struck. We were leaning toward the unsub being a friend to his victims, but Howell's abduction appeared incongruous. Prior victims were charged twenty-some years ago. Howell was charged within the last six months. The other thing that hit me was her wording *big shot*. Lyons had told Paige that Gene had gotten off his charges because "he knew someone who knew someone." We had considered that someone to be Hogan's father, the mayor. What if it was Larson? His primary concern seemed to lie with his paper. Conflict made for terrific headlines. But how much clout would an editor have? And how long had Larson been such? Did our killer sacrifice his scruples to get someone off, only to repay him in kind?

"Your boyfriend beat the animal abuse charges against him," I stated.

"Yes, because the right thing is always done."

"What do you mean by that exactly?" I had to be careful how I articulated those words.

"Just that. Justice was done, Agent. It might not be what you would see as justice, but the right thing always plays out."

I imagined the future when she could be receiving notice that Howell had been murdered. Would she still feel that justice had played out?

"How did Larson react to the charges against Mr. Howell?"

Seconds of silence passed.

"Melissa?" I prompted.

"He was kind of weird. You know what writers are like I'm sure. They're usually in their own world."

"How was he weird?" Jack asked directly.

"He was supportive but distant at the same time."

"Does Larson have a dog?"

"Oh, he used to. Her name was Molly."

Chapter 44

We left with the knowledge Howell was a close friend of Saul Larson. Coincidence? I didn't think so. The only thing that didn't line up with that reasoning was why choose Howell when he had, up until recently, been choosing victims from further back? Was it to get us looking at Brent Turner? First, frame Fields, now Turner?

Jack was driving, another cigarette in his mouth—of course—and I made the call to Jenna Simpson. She answered on the third ring.

"Oh, you're the young agent? Hello. I was wondering if you'd call."

I pictured Paige glaring at me and lighting me on fire with the intent of her stare. I stayed focused on business. "I have a question for you."

"Shoot." Jenna's voice carried a smile.

"Was your husband friends with Saul Larson?"

"Oh, and here I thought you were going to ask me out for drinks."

"Jenna, maybe another time."

Jack glanced over at me. I needed his attention back on the road. We were coming up on the rear end of another SUV.

"You want to make a girl beg, Mr. Agent?"

I cleared my throat. "Saul Larson?"

"What about him?"

"Was your husband friends with him?"

"What's in it for me?"

I realized all of the women involved with these men weren't too heartbroken by their absence, but then again, if they abused an innocent dog, they weren't men worth missing. "You could help us find your husband's killer."

"You think Saul did this? You think he killed Darren?" Panic and anger replaced any prior inclination to seduce me into her bed.

"So, he was a friend of your husband's?"

"Yeah, distant friends. I think he was at the bar on Wednesdays sometimes. Darren mentioned seeing him."

"At Smitty's Bar?"

"Yes." A second's pause. "Hey, what about our drinks?"

"I'll be in touch." I hung up immediately. I didn't need to give her proposal the trace of a thought or I might surrender to male weakness.

I updated Jack. "They were friends."

"This is getting to be more than coincidence. Call Nadia. Have her specifically search for Saul Larson among the bar's receipts."

"On it."

I contacted Nadia through the onboard system, and seconds later we had our answer. Larson was a confirmed regular at Smitty's Bar. By extension, it was easy to assume that Saul Larson and Darren Simpson could have been drinking buddies.

CHAPTER 45

ALL OF US WERE AT Denver PD poring over the evidence from the Bailey case and sharing our discoveries.

"Bailey worked for Larson's father," Paige said.

I noticed that Zachery had his face in crime scene photographs and he seemed to be going back and forth between a couple of them.

"We confirmed that Simpson and Howell were friends with Larson. Larson had a dog," I offered.

"We need more," Jack said.

"I don't understand how much more we need." I should have backed down, as evidenced by Zachery looking up from the photos to Jack then to me. "We moved on Bowen and Fields with less."

"The guy had a pickup truck, access to the victims, Brandon. He was looking solid for the murders. Larson has circumstantial against him right now."

"Larson knew at least two of the victims. He had knowledge of these animal abuse cases, he shared a background with Fields. They went to the same university, at the same time. He easily could have framed Fields, and then tried to do the same with Turner, only it didn't work. He acted prematurely."

"Hmm."

That one wasn't in my favor. He didn't appreciate my standing up to him, but this was something I felt strongly about. We needed to get Larson now and give Howell a fighting chance of survival. "Why are we leaving Howell's life in danger?"

"It's quite likely he's already dead, Brandon," Paige said.

Was I the only one who was not giving up hope? "What happened to your speech, Jack, about no one else dying?"

Jack wouldn't even grant me eye contact.

"Pending, our unsub has moved up his game. He's killed three people in a week. He's not going to slow down now."

"So that's it? We assume he's already dead and just give up on trying to save him?"

"You think Larson's so damn guilty, Kid, get us something to move on."

I was so angry, and based on the heat in my earlobes they were a bright red. The hair on the back of my neck stood on end. I reached for some photographs. "What forensic evidence were they able to pull from Bailey?"

"Not much of anything. Not much from the scene either. What you see is what you get." Paige gestured across the table to a few pieces of broken glass, a spiked dog choker, and some articles of clothing—all of the items were sealed in bags.

I focused on the picture I had taken from the pile and my eyes fell upon Bailey's body. Leave it to me to pick one of the corpse.

"The cause of death resulted from being beaten?" I asked.

"Yes."

"What are these?" I pointed to what looked like holes all around the victim's neck. They were spread out at even intervals.

"Puncture wounds. The ME concluded the cause of death was a blow to the head. It wasn't looked into any further."

"Wasn't looked into any further? The guy's found sealed up in a wall and it's not pursued from every angle. Who even handled this case?"

There was the clearing of a throat and McClellan stood in the doorway.

"Just thought I'd see if you needed anything."

"You're the one who investigated the case when Bailey's body was found?"

"Yes, I was."

There was something there…right on the tip of my mind. I looked across the table. My eyes settled on the choker. I took some photos from Zachery's hands of the original scene, back twenty-six years ago when Bailey had gone missing, and there it was.

"I think I know what made those puncture wounds. Our killer strangled Bailey with that," I butted my head toward the choker, "to finish him off."

"You're forgetting blunt force trauma to the head."

"I still think our unsub may have strangled him to finish things off."

"After all those years, any physical evidence—bruising, for example—would have disappeared so it is possible," Zachery added. "Also the tiny bones in his neck may have been broken, but this wasn't noted in the autopsy report."

"Our killer started back then." Revelation dawned on Paige's face.

"Was the spiked choker run for prints?"

The detective pulled out on the knot of his tie. "No…we had no idea the guy was murdered with it. We didn't even have a body when all this was collected, remember?"

"The evidence was here all this time, you just had to go back twenty-six years."

McClellan looked like he was going to be sick.

"Detective, we need you to take this to your lab immediately. Run it for prints and compare them against the ones pulled from the hate mail, specifically the ones that were tame and generic," Jack said. "Also, compare it to the partial pulled from the duct tape and prints from Ellis's door. Paige, go with him and set things up with Nadia to help get this done."

"On it."

They left the room.

Jack got up and paced a few steps. "We need a personal trigger that would have set Larson off, something to connect Larson to Bailey's dog."

"One second, Boss." Zachery shuffled through a bunch of paper and pulled out a sheet. "German Shepard and its name was Molly. Of course, just as I remembered."

Jack and I looked at each other. I spoke first.

"Howell's girlfriend said Molly was the name of Larson's dog. I know there's no way it's the same dog, but is it just a coincidence that it's named the same thing?"

"You're thinking that Larson killed Bailey and took his dog? Then got a successor—or more than one—and named it the same thing?" Zachery asked.

I shrugged my shoulders. "Why not?"

"I can't believe I missed something like this."

McClellan stood with Paige behind their lab tech, frowning like a disciplined child.

"You know we had no reason to even pick this choker up twenty-six years ago."

Paige didn't know what he expected from her. Was he looking for praise for a job well done? She couldn't extend it. She couldn't think of anything to say that would soothe his conscience. When Bailey's body had been discovered, the evidence from twenty-six years ago should have been scoured with microscopic intensity.

As if reading her mind, McClellan defended himself. "My superior at the time was in a rush to close the case. Twenty years had already passed. I don't know, I don't have an excuse. I just figured any leads would be dead."

McClellan seemed to have the compulsion to keep speaking. An inclination Paige recognized as him trying to tamp down the guilt he was feeling over his negligence. The nonstop talk was annoying and counter-productive though. She had to offer him something so that they had quiet to work.

"Sometimes things are not clear until later on when you look from a fresh perspective."

McClellan nodded but flushed. He recognized her efforts to pacify him.

The lab technician, who had been on the phone with Nadia, addressed Paige. "She wants to speak with you."

"Nadia."

"We've got the killer, Paige."

"Slow down. One thing at a time."

"The prints from the choker match the partial from the tape."

Paige didn't understand why Nadia was so confident they, in turn, would match to Larson. "I'm still not understanding."

"That's because I haven't told you everything. Saul Larson's uncle is the one who owns the garage."

"The one that…" Paige couldn't finish.

"That's right. The origin point that Ellis was dragged from."

"Hogan said that the owners go away in the winter."

"It doesn't mean they wouldn't have given a key to their favorite nephew to check on things while they are away."

Something wasn't right here. Had the detectives known all along? If so, why not bring it up when they turned their suspicions to Larson?

"Thank you, Nadia."

"No problem, but that's not all. Remember the chrome paint found at Ellis's crime scene?"

"Of course."

"The results tie back to Chevrolet and GMC pickups and what they offer under their trailering package. Saul Larson has a GMC Sierra that falls into that category."

Chapter 46

Everything would turn out better than the Advocate had imagined. The detour had been worth it if only for infusing lifeblood into his work. He had a feeling that the feds would be digging into his past with intense vigor and determination, but he still saw himself coming out the victor.

He had failed at so much in life, but things were changing to his favor. With the execution of justice he had overcome any bars placed in front of him. And if he had ever been questioned about his life's direction twenty-six years ago, the standard response would have spewed from his mouth—the programmed one that conformed to manmade guidelines. But he didn't need them to tell him what he could do, or how he should live his life.

He set his focus on the recent Offender. He was doing this one just for fun. This one wouldn't affect him as the last one had.

The prior son of a bitch was responsible for his hand looking and hurting the way it did, but he remained strong, steadied, and focused on what needed to be done. He had bandaged it up and told himself out of sight and out of mind. When a twinge of pain radiated from it, he let it go, dismissing it as he had the man who died.

The cell he was using for this Offender was perfect. He had used it once before, and the excruciating pain it inflicted was death-dealing.

The Advocate had made it with his own two hands.

Utilizing a local company and a big chain home improvement store, the glass box was complete with a space heater. He ensured that it was out of his captive's reach. To make the man even more uncomfortable, he had heat lamps shining in from four sides. He had mounted a camera in the top corner to watch the man wither to death.

This means of execution was one of the longer tortures he meted out, but it would equal full atonement for the man's sins.

The man's screams had gone mute. No doubt his throat was parched. His organs would be failing him soon.

The Advocate would be there to witness it all unfold. He sat back and relaxed.

Chapter 47

We finally had enough to move in on Larson. He used to have a dog named Molly, just like Bailey had and had lived in the neighborhood at the same time as Bailey's murder. If that wasn't enough, Bailey worked for Larson's father's construction company.

Larson had a connection to and reason to hate and frame Fields. He would have had an intimate knowledge of the animal abuse cases. He had volunteered with the animal shelter and attempted to strangle a man who had abused an animal. And, the latest results, he owned a GMC Sierra that could be connected to the chrome paint found at Ellis's crime scene and his uncle owned the garage. Paige and agents from the local field office and officers from PD stood vigilant there while they waited for the warrant to come through. Jack, Zachery, and I headed to Larson's home, with additional backup, as we already had the necessary clearance for there.

Local PD confirmed that Larson was home and we were getting ready to move in. The pickup was tucked away in the garage.

I banged on the front door. Jack stood beside me.

"FBI, open up!"

Zachery was around the back side of Larson's house with a local agent.

Squad cars had cordoned off the street. A couple was in front of the place, being used as shields to the officers who held their guns ready to fire.

"Open up! FBI!" I banged again.

Footsteps inside the house vibrated the front porch.

The door handle twisted. I steadied my weapon and both of us had our guns trained on Larson when he opened the door.

"What are you do—"

I spun him around and worked at getting cuffs on him. "You are under arrest for the murder—"

"Are you kidding me? What are you talking about?"

Jack pressed the arrest warrant against Larson's torso, and with both hands secured behind his back, the papers fell to the floor.

I handed Larson over to an agent from the local field office and hurried through the house.

"Where is Howell?"

Larson had an odd grin on his face.

"Never mind, we'll find him."

We worked our way through the house. Calls of "All clear" kept working their way over the coms.

I went back to Larson, who was being held inside his front door. I grabbed him by the collar of his shirt and pulled him up to meet my face. "Where is he?"

"This is going to make one interesting story."

I tightened my grip. "Do you think this is funny? That it's a joke?"

"Let him go, Brandon," Jack ordered.

I let Larson go, reluctantly.

Jack swooped past me and pulled Larson to a couch and threw him down.

Any amusement over the situation had left Larson's face. Anger replaced it.

"Where is Howell?"

"You don't know what you're talking about, do you?"

"I'm not asking again."

"You think I killed those people?" Larson laughed. "I was never popular, but I didn't resort to killing." Hysteria took over and had tears pouring down his cheeks.

Jack shook him. "You used to have a dog named Molly."

"Is that a crime?"

"Ken Bailey was murdered in this neighborhood twenty-six

years ago."

"Good for him."

"You did it. Did he kill Molly? Is that why you killed him?"

Larson's face paled.

"Speak, Larson. You're facing multiple counts of—"

"I think I know who the killer is." Larson's tongue sounded thick as if he barely held down bile.

"Agent Harper?" A local field agent came into the living room.

"The pickup's clear. There's no damage to the hitch."

"You think I dragged Ellis with my truck?" Larson shook his head fiercely. "It wasn't me. But I told you. I think I know who did it."

My cell rang and it was Paige. The warrant had come through for the garage. "I'd be wiping that smirk off your face, Larson. We've got you."

"I can't believe he'd do this, but then again, life wasn't kind to him until a few years back when he won the lottery. Before that, as an adult, he didn't amount to much." Larson mumbled almost incoherently.

"Did you hear him, Larson? Time is up," Jack said.

"Gregory Ford."

"That's Bailey's cousin," Zachery said.

Larson looked past Jack to Zachery. "That's right."

"Why would he kill his cousin?"

"That's the best part right there." Larson chewed the inside of his lip. He swallowed and his eyes sought out mine. "Bailey killed Ford's dog when they were both kids."

"He killed his cousin's dog?"

"Yeah, I saw it with my own eyes. It was horrible. Ken had it hanging from the leash and walked it right up to Greg. He was laughing as he did it."

"Shit." The word escaped my lips.

Zachery stepped forward a few feet. "Why name the dog you had Molly?"

"That was the name of Greg's dog. The one that was killed. It affected more than one kid. I wasn't moved to retaliation."

"What about your uncle's garage?" I asked, on a hunch.

"What about it?"

"Is there any way that Gregory Ford would have access to it?"

"Yeah, of course. I gave him a key years ago. During the winter months, I know he goes there and tinkers."

"Son of a bitch." Jack was on his phone as he rushed from the house.

Chapter 48

THEY HAD RECEIVED THE ALL CLEAR, but Paige's feet remained grounded. She assessed the amount of fire power around her. Between the local field agents and PD officers, they could have blown the garage into the sky. But, she was in charge here and they would do things her way. If they moved too quickly, lives could be needlessly lost.

"All right, we go in—front and back. Split up and keep on guard." She took one step and her phone rang. Its trill had her heart thumping. The men stopped all movement and looked at her. She should have had the volume off, but ID confirmed it was a call she needed to answer. "Jack?"

His message caused her stomach to swirl. They were now after a man by the name of Gregory Ford. He wasn't at his home. That meant only one thing.

In the building, mere feet away there was a serial killer and, likely, his latest victim. Something about getting to this point never got easier. To face the monsters who inflicted torture and murder was always a surreal encounter—a sick darkness hung in the air and threatened to suffocate her.

While still on the line with Jack, she heard the ding of an incoming message and guessed it was a picture of Ford.

"We're on it, Boss." She hung up, hoping that her training didn't fail her in this time of need.

"YOU KNOW YOUR ACTIONS BROUGHT THIS UPON YOU," the Advocate said through the speaker system he had installed.

"What?"

He laughed. "You're kidding me. You don't know why you're here. You are obtuse. You hurt and killed an innocent dog. They are man's best friend. You took his trust and twisted it to your advantage. You worked out your satanic thoughts."

Nothing.

"What, no response?"

Sweat glistened on the Offender's body. His clothing was soaking wet. His body swayed and he opted to sit down on the floor.

"It won't be long and you'll have paid for your sins."

"WE GO IN ON MY MARK," Paige said.

One of the local agents had already picked the lock. Paige raised three fingers and when all were down, they breached the garage.

She followed. "FBI!"

Inside, it was dimly lit but there was a GMC Sierra pickup. As the agents and officers spread out in the space, she went to the vehicle. Crouched near the trailer hitch, she swept her flashlight over it. Chrome paint was missing.

Her heart beat against her ribs. Adrenaline fused with fear but initialized forward momentum.

"We've got the right guy." A voice came over the comms and it must have been one of the local agents. "There's a shrine out back for a dog named Molly."

That's not all they had. She hurried through the building, sweeping her light in large arcs as she moved. Her eyes caught something.

The other agents moved around, clearing the bays, but her attention was on a door. It sat crooked on its hinges and was slightly open. As she moved toward it, she had that sinking feeling. What would she find when she opened it? It didn't appear access a room on the main level. A basement? Below ground never held anything good. She pushed through her trepidation. She owed it to the reputation of Jack's team.

She swung it open, her attention steadied ahead of her, but she heard others rush behind her. She balanced her gun and the flashlight, but it was no longer needed. A bright glow illuminated the base of the stairs. She moved toward the light.

There was a man in a glass box. He looked near death, but it wasn't Howell.

Ford stood to the side of him, and when he saw her, lifted his gun on the man.

Paige held her firearm steady. "Put down your weapon."

Ford shook his head. "He is guilty and needs to pay for what he's done."

Paige's eyes went to the man. If they didn't get him out of there soon, this wouldn't be a rescue anymore. "I said put down your weapon."

Ford smirked and twisted his body to face the man.

She heard agents and officers come down the stairs behind her. She squeezed the trigger.

The bullet struck Ford in his arm, causing his hand to release his weapon.

"No," he cried while cradling his wound. "He must pay!"

He was a man gone mad, the look in his eyes burrowed into Paige's mind. He took fast steps toward the box and the heater.

"Stop!" Paige solidified her stance. She was prepared to shoot him again. The placement of this one would inflict more damage.

She knew all the other law enforcement personnel around her had their guns readied and aimed on Ford as well. If she wanted Ford to survive to pay for his crimes, she'd have to figure out a way to talk the situation down.

She lowered her weapon. "I can understand why you don't like these men."

Ford stopped moving. "I hate them."

"For what they do to their animals, they need to pay."

"Yes. I am the Advocate for the Defenseless."

This man had managed to give full logic to his actions. His assigned terms further confirmed his justification. "But what if they are innocent?"

"The Offenders are not!" He swooped to the floor, his good arm reaching for his weapon.

The bullet caught him in the upper chest and jolted him back.

His eyes enlarged as he collapsed to the floor. His gaze, as it fell on Paige, held great sadness.

A local field agent, who had fired the last round, secured Ford, while others rushed to get the man out of the box.

"Paige."

She spun to see Brandon coming down the stairs and the rest of the team following behind him. Their faces were a welcome sight among this hell hole.

INVESTIGATORS WORKED OVER THE GARAGE AND ITS PROPERTY. It seemed Ford did more than "tinker" there. Dogs were brought in and bodies were uncovered in the back. I had no doubt they would be Garner and Ball from years ago. A freezer in the basement held the bodies of Lyons, and someone they guessed to be Howell—the latter was deformed by acid.

The man in the glass box was Marshall Quinn and he was a prick...maybe it was the heat? When we freed him, he had said 'about time.' I had a feeling being a jerk was in his nature as no one had reported him missing.

It was later confirmed that Ford had rented a red Nissan and this is what he used when kidnapping Ellis. Although he could have afforded to buy his own as Ford had won the lottery two years back, netting himself a few million after taxes. So even if he didn't know each of his victims, they could have recognized his face from the paper or the local news. His background showed he had attended Stanford University, the same as Fields and Larson, but never graduated. He went on to take odd jobs but never settled in a career.

A hunch I had paid off when I called Nadia to inquire about Simpson's drinking buddies. Ford drank on Wednesdays like Simpson and Larson. Nadia also found out that Ford's mother worked for Denver PD at the time Lyons was charged. Coincidently, she was the one who wrote up the charges against him.

"I still can't believe Ford had his mother get rid of the charges against Lyons," I said.

"Ford wanted to be the one to exact punishment, not the courts," Paige said. "Typically all they get are some monetary fines and brief probations. Ford wanted more for Lyons, for all of them."

I wondered why Ford had waited so long to act out against Lyons—or against any of them for that matter. Maybe it was to place more distance between him and them? He must have been able to resist the urge to kill, at first. I wondered what had triggered him to start again.

Ford was questioned in his hospital room and he never bothered to deny the allegations. He said it was Ken Bailey's fault for killing his dog as a kid. Ford had never forgotten.

He had said, "When I showed up at that house, a dog tied up on a short leash to the back deck, out in the freezing cold of winter, and he answered the door. He deserved it." Ford nodded. "Yes, he deserved it. I knew then what I had to do with my life."

"Why frame Fields?" Jack asked.

Ford laughed. "He took everything away from me. I was trying to turn my life around. He stole the credit for the papers I wrote. He got that job I deserved with the paper because he cheated his way through life. I hoped he would go down for this, but he got what he earned in the end anyway—death. Then I thought I'd frame that kid at the paper, Turner. It was even better when you looked at Larson. The guy's a real loser. The sucker actually thought we were friends." A sick smile lit his face. "That night I killed Ken, I was working on what would have been the best piece I'd ever written."

"Ken Bailey was your cousin." I don't know why I attempted to appeal to his humanity.

It warranted a shrug. "We didn't stay in touch. He never even recognized me when I was at his door. Family isn't based on blood and species."

"Why did you start killing again in two thousand nine?"

"Who said I stopped?"

The truth was in his eyes. He was attempting to mislead me into thinking he had continued killing after Bailey, but our investigation didn't show any evidence of that. "Why Dean Garner?"

"I was rethinking my life and realized I had nothing going

for me. Nothing at all. Then I remembered what I was good at. When I took Ken's life, I felt justified and had made a difference. I remembered reading about Garner in the paper. It was time for him to pay."

Something still wasn't settling for me. Garner was two thousand and nine. Ball was one year later, but his recent victims followed after four years, taking place in rapid succession.

"You try to control your urge to kill."

His gaze drifted from mine and it told me more than if he had made eye contact. Along with his refusal to look at me, he chewed on his bottom lip, like a scared child. Finally, he spoke. "No. Fate intervened that night. I wasn't meant to be a writer. I was meant to exact justice for the victims who have no voice, for the defenseless. I am their advocate. You can quote me on that."

Chapter 49

We were going to make it back in time for Christmas after all. The paperwork was still in progress, but it would all be sorted out in plenty of time.

We were waiting to board our flight and sitting in an airport lobby designed for passengers of charter aircraft. Sitting there, I had mixed feelings about returning home. I had nothing waiting for me but a finalized divorce.

I glanced over at Paige, who had said very little to me since that night at the bar, and I took the blame for that.

She sat slumped in a chair, wearing the cream sweater from the other night. Her red curls hung down. She must have sensed me watching her. She returned my gaze.

I mouthed *Can I come over* and she nodded.

She had her bag and coat on the seat to her right. I sat in the one to her left.

"It looks like you'll be home in plenty of time to celebrate."

She smiled, but there was sadness that lurked in the shadows. "I will be. I'm happy about that. I think Mom would have killed me if I missed the family dinner." She paused, picking at her sweater. "What about you? Are you going to be all right?"

Just like Paige, always concerned about my wellbeing. "Yeah, I'm going to be good. Better than good. Howell's girlfriend spread the positive attitude."

Her brows scrunched together, and I told her about the woman who was high on happiness.

"As long as it works for her." She didn't look at me when she said that, but ahead and out through the glass to the tarmac.

"About the other night."

She turned to me. "No, Brandon, don't worry about it."

"I'm not worried about it, but I am sorry."

She studied my eyes.

"I shouldn't have let you leave before telling you that I love you too."

Her chin quivered and her eyes misted.

"I should have told you that a long time ago. I'm just afraid of it."

"The big, bad Brandon is afraid of love?" She smiled, and I sensed it was to suppress the urge to cry.

"I am afraid of loving you." I glanced over at Jack and Zachery, who were into some serious conversation, based on the sharp angles of Jack's face.

She pulled down on her sweater. "I know what you mean. We'd risk our careers."

My insides were tearing apart. It was reminiscent of the day Deb had called me to say our marriage was over. Here, I had another woman I loved, but I had to let her go.

"You fought hard to get where you are," I said.

"And you're just starting out."

I narrowed my eyes. "A dig at the new kid?"

She laughed and swatted at me. "You know what I mean."

"I do."

"So, what are we going to do about it, about how we feel for each other?"

I heard it in the tone of her voice. Her heart was breaking like mine.

"I think we have to see other people, Paige." The words, the acknowledgment, sent splinters of pain through my heart.

She didn't say anything. Her eyes remained locked with mine. "It's how it has to be, Brandon." She swallowed roughly and tucked a strand of hair behind an ear. "It's for the best."

"Yeah."

We both went quiet, unsure of what to say to each other. There really was nothing left to say.

I faced her. "It's always bad timing with us, isn't it?"

"Well, the first time you were married." She smirked and her eyes carried an evil glint. "And now it's either us or the careers we love."

"Yep, life stinks."

She touched my forearm. I wanted to do nothing more than pull her in and take her mouth. To whisk her back to the hotel room and hold her until morning—

"Friends?"

I smiled. "Always."

"What are you doing for Christmas?"

Note to Readers

If you've enjoyed this novel, please tell your friends and family about it. If you have time to write a brief, honest review on the retailer site where you purchased this book that, too, is appreciated.

Carolyn loves to hear from her readers. You can reach her at carolyn@carolynarnold.net.

Upon receipt of your e-mail, you will be added to her newsletter mailing unless you express your desire otherwise.

Keep on reading for a sample of *Blue Baby*, book 4 in the Brandon Fisher FBI series.

Do you, or have you, worked in law enforcement?

If so, Carolyn would love to know how you thought she did when it came to the police procedure in this story. Her goal is to provide the most realistic and entertaining police procedural novels in the marketplace. Your feedback would be much appreciated. Please e-mail her at the address noted above.

Read on for an exciting preview of Carolyn Arnold's next thrilling novel featuring Brandon Fisher

BLUE BABY

THE WHITE SILK WAS DRAPED over the porcelain of the tub like angel wings. She was beautiful, radiant. Her face was flushed, and her eyes were open and staring at him.

He took the set of fake lashes from his pocket and applied them. He coated her eyeball with glue before delicately using both hands to pull her eyes closed. The extensions fanned against her flesh.

He applied the eye shadow and stepped back to appreciate the hues of brown and gold.

Next. Lipstick.

He smeared the tube across her lips. The bright red was an exquisite touch of color against her fair skin. He put the veil in place and wisped back the nylon until it framed her face and ensconced her shoulders. He stood back to admire his work thus far.

Divine.

The blonde sat with her back against the end of the tub, her dress spilling down her frame and over the ledge. Her hair was a bed of curls beneath her veil. Her makeup appeared professional, and he was pleased with his hard work. He wasn't nearly as perfect with the first one.

Her mouth carried a hint of peace. Of happiness.

The Big Event was under way.

"Almost."

His gaze went to her left hand resting in her lap.

How could he have been so foolish? Was he rushing things? He moved swiftly through her apartment and found what he sought on her dresser.

"There you go, beautiful." He slipped the wedding ring on her finger, leaving him with one final task.

He took the cigar cutter from his pocket, slipped her ring finger into it, and squeezed. As he had the first time, he marveled at the ease of it, how such small blades were able to cut through bone. He let the severed finger fall against her ivory dress.

Stepping back, he took in her beauty.

She was pleased. It was in the way her lips were set.

He smiled. "Now, you can just be happy."

CHAPTER 1

HER SNORING HAD KEPT ME up for most of the night, but I wasn't cruel enough to wake her. While I had considered pinching her nose to quiet her, I mustered the restraint not to. I didn't really want to deal with a sleep-deprived *and* pissed-off woman.

The solution wasn't in getting sleep myself—it was already five AM—it would be in downing a pot of coffee. I'd need that much to function today. But thanks to technology, I'd have to repeat the coffee-brewing process twelve times since I'd upgraded to one of those single-serve makers. I put in the pod, and after some protest in the form of moaning and gurgling, the machine sputtered out the black nectar into my waiting cup. While the brew finished, I rested my eyes. I'd have to be alert soon enough.

The text message had come in overnight, bathing the bedroom in a white glow. I had read it, careful not to tug the sheets and wake my female companion. The gist was that another sicko had decided to use the world as his demented playground. I didn't know the details yet, but the summation was always a variation of that fact, and my presence had been requested in the briefing room first thing.

I breathed in, eyes closed, my nose appreciating the robust aroma that filled the air while my mind drifted to last night. It might have been a bad idea inviting her over, but it had been fun. I'd have to wake her soon, but I'd put it off for as long as possible.

The puttering of the coffeemaker came to an end, and I added two lumps of sugar and some milk to my cup.

"Brandon? What are you doing up so early?"

She was in one my shirts, her hair tousled over her shoulders. The way she was winding one strand around her finger would drive any man mad.

Forget the coffee. Forget the snoring. There were some sacrifices worth making.

"There's a case." God, she looked good, but I dared not touch her.

She slipped her arms around my waist, and I continued to fight the impulse to scoop her up and take her back to my bed. "But you had the day booked off. We had plans."

"I know, but sometimes these things happen." *Maybe a little embrace wouldn't hurt anything.* I wrapped my arms around her and slapped her butt.

She let out a yelp. "Be careful what you're starting." She snuggled her face into my neck, her tongue teasing my flesh.

"We'll have to take a rain check," I said, then cupped her face and tilted it upward until her mouth met mine. My jaw was tight, determined, and hungry. I took her without mercy. She reciprocated with as much as I gave. Slipping my hand under the shirt she wore, I found her breasts and teased her nipples with the pads of my thumbs. She let out a moan and arched her head back.

God, I loved giving her pleasure as much as I loved receiving it. I parted from her only long enough to clear a space on the counter and then lifted her up.

Her perfume filled my head, diluting all logic and intoxicating my senses. I trailed kisses from her neck down to her chest and slid a taut nipple between my teeth.

Her deep breathing encouraged me, and the hardening of her nipple reciprocated what was happening in my pants.

Forget work.

As I parted her legs, my cell phone rang. "Son of a bitch!"

"I had a feeling it was too good to be true." She tapped a kiss on my cheek and hopped down from the counter.

The caller ID flashed Paige Dawson. I took a deep breath. No big deal. Paige was a beautiful redhead with electric-green eyes, who had me straying from my marriage while at the training academy.

It was only by a strange twist of fate that I had wound up on the same team as her within the Behavioral Analysis Unit of the FBI. When my divorce had been finalized in December, Paige and I had determined that a relationship between us wasn't going to work. The age difference between us had never mattered. She was in her early forties, and I was twenty-nine. What had interfered were our careers.

I answered with my gaze on the new woman in my life—Becky Tulson. We'd met last fall when I was working on a case in Dumfries, Virginia. The attraction had been instant and the conversation between us stimulating, but until recently, the situation had been complicated.

"Brandon," Paige said, "there's been a change of plans."

A banging came from the front door immediately after, and Becky nodded to me before heading off to answer it.

What the hell? The place was becoming Grand Central, and all I needed was another twenty minutes to fit in a quick one. Apparently I was asking for too much.

"What's going on?" I asked into the receiver.

"Brandon," Becky called to me, "Jack's here." She stood behind the opened door, shielding her body from Jack's line of sight.

"We're outside," Paige said.

"It's a little too late to tell me that." I hung up, wondering how it was possible for this day to descend downhill any faster than it already was.

I hurried to the front door, experiencing a moment of awkwardness. My boss and my lover, face-to-face. My lover wearing only a shirt. My shirt.

"Don't stand there, kid. We have a flight to catch. Grab your go bag."

"One second, Jack." I closed the door on him and worked to get my house key off the ring. I handed it to Becky. "Leave when you're ready."

She pouted but nodded. She understood. She also worked in law enforcement and could appreciate that if the job called, one had to respond.

"I don't know how long I'll be gone. Heck, I'm not even sure where I'm headed."

"No worries." She smiled and kissed my lips. I lingered. She pulled back. "You better get going. Jack doesn't strike me as the patient type."

"You have no idea." I grabbed the bag I kept by the front door—for the very purpose of last-minute trips like this—and opened the door. Jack was still standing there, and I jumped, having expected him to be in the car by now.

"I thought we were meeting at—"

Jack shook his head. "There's a new development."

A "new development" meant the case we were going to discuss had become urgent. It meant someone else was dead. And our cases rarely involved run-of-the-mill shootings or passionate kills in the heat of the moment.

We hunted psychotic unsubs.

Chapter 2

We were at thirty thousand feet being briefed on the case. The plane was taking us to Grand Forks, the third largest city in North Dakota. It was an hour away from Fargo and had a population of over fifty thousand.

Nadia Webber was patched through on a video call from Quantico, and from the looks of the monitors behind her, she was about to share information most people were better off not knowing. But this was what I had signed up for. Although I had originally seen myself in a counterterrorism unit, the first available opening was in the Behavioral Analysis Unit. But it provided me the opportunity to stop those responsible for grievous acts. The job also allowed me to tap into the minds of killers and discover what moved them to do what they did. While most people carried on unaware of the true evil in the world, I had never preferred naïveté. I favored knowledge, and second to that, action.

Loading onto the jet first thing on a Monday morning was one way to get the week started quickly, if not abruptly.

As another member of the team, Zachery joined us. He was a certified genius. Everything he read in a textbook during university was available for speedy recall. But his big brain never got in the way of his being a goof. He was eight years older than me.

Paige, Zachery, and I sucked back on coffee. Jack was the only exception.

I thought of Becky standing in my kitchen wearing nothing but my shirt. All I'd needed was another twenty minutes. God, I hated leaving her behind. We'd had plans to go out for a nice dinner, too. Even though it had been more her idea than mine. I never understood meals equating to entertainment. I was into nourishing my body and moving on.

I caught Paige glancing at me again, and I had a feeling she was well aware that I had moved on. It was even possible she saw Becky answer my door. She had met Becky on the same investigation I had.

"This has got to be one of the saddest cases we've worked," Nadia began.

"Without the commentary adlib, Nadia," Jack said, coaxing her along.

He liked news presented without narrative flair. It was about getting the information and stopping the bad guy. Not much seemed to affect the man, but instead of envying him that, I pitied him for it.

"Yes, Jack, of course," Nadia went on. "We have two victims. The latest was discovered yesterday."

Pictures of a woman came on the screen to Nadia's left: a pretty blonde with gray eyes. Her makeup was tastefully applied and a dusting of freckles graced the bridge of her nose. She wore silver hoops, and from the snapshot, I'd guess she had a love for fashion.

"This is Tara Day," Nadia continued. "She was twenty-five. Local police arrived on scene at nine AM yesterday. They found her in her apartment after a coworker, Glen Little, called it in. He said that he was there to pick her up for work. They were putting in overtime for a client."

"What did she do for a living?" Paige asked.

"Tara was a clerk for a local accounting firm. The overtime still needs to be verified, but the coworker's background check was clean."

Lack of a criminal record meant little at times. It could simply mean that he just hadn't been caught in the past.

Another picture of Tara appeared on the screen. This one was of her in a wedding gown in her bathtub. Her hands were folded over each other in her lap, sitting in a pool of blood.

"Our unsub cuts off their ring fingers and leaves it in their laps,"

Nadia said.

"I find it strange he doesn't take them as trophies." Paige angled her cup and set it down when she seemed to realize it was empty.

"As nice as that sounds, there's no indication our guy takes a trophy. At least none we've discovered."

"You mentioned he's done this before?" Zachery prodded.

"Correct. One year ago to the day. Her name was Cheryl Bradley. Age twenty-four."

Zachery snapped the tab down on the lid of his cup. "So he kills on the summer solstice. Some religious connection? Must have some importance to our unsub. The women's ages are close, too."

"What about sexual assault?" Paige asked.

Nadia shook her head. "Nothing indicates either victim had sexual relations within twelve hours of death."

"And the cause of death?" Jack tapped an unlit cigarette against the table. I knew what his immediate plans were once he got off the plane.

Nadia fanned her pen between two fingers. "Suffocation. He gets on top of his victims and places his knee in their solar plexus."

"Compressive asphyxia," Zachery jumped in, showing off his abundance of knowledge. "Not a nice way to go."

Nadia showed us a picture of a brunette with brown eyes. "This is Cheryl Bradley. She worked as a receptionist for a graphic design company. At first glance, the two victims seem to have two things in common besides cause of death: age range and location. They live within three blocks of each other."

The image morphed into one of Cheryl in a bathtub, and it was rather eerie the way it resembled that of Tara, despite the differences in their coloring.

Zachery leaned forward. "He's likely someone from the area, then."

I narrowed my eyes at the photo. Cheryl's hands lay on top of each other as Tara's did. "The way he poses them with care afterward speaks of a connection or bond with his victims," I added. "He chooses them for a specific reason."

"The ring finger being cut off may show betrayal or heartache."

This was from Paige. "It's also possible he could be striving to recreate an event."

"You're alluding to a dead woman in a bathtub? It doesn't sound like a common thing. But, if so, when and who?" The question slipped out. I knew it was essentially rhetorical at this point. There wasn't an answer yet to provide. "Did our unsub witness someone carry out a murder like this or find a woman's body? Were there victims before Cheryl?"

"Nothing in the system comes back similar to these two cases," Nadia said.

"At the very least, he is selective and organized. He waits a year between victims. He doesn't need to kill but is moved to do so." Zachery expanded on the brainstorming. "He experienced a deep hurt at some point. Like Paige said, a woman may have betrayed him. He can't move past the pain and that's why he severs their fingers. These women could have hurt their fiancés. And June is the most popular month for weddings. All of this is best guess. The women might not have been engaged."

"Nadia, who did the police suspect for Cheryl's murder?" Jack asked.

"Their prime suspect was her ex-fiancé. Phil Payne broke it off."

"Did he say why?"

"He said Cheryl was a flirt."

"And his alibi for the time of her murder?"

"This is where you have to love the irony. He was with another woman. She swore under oath she spent the night with him."

"What about the latest victim, Tara Day? Was she engaged?" I asked. Maybe it was a stupid question based on the ring on her finger, but it was also possible the killer brought it and placed it there.

"Taking the ring and dress into consideration, one would assume so. Police haven't tracked him down yet, though, and there are no indications in Tara's apartment that she was in a relationship. Like I said, I'm afraid the only glaring similarities, besides their murders, are their vicinity and age range."

"Nadia, find out if Glen Little crossed paths with the first victim during previous employment or otherwise."

"You got it."

"Thanks, Nadia. Make sure you send anything else on these cases our way immediately."

The monitor went black. I observed the sharp lines of Jack's features. His intention, like the rest of the team's, was to find the man who had murdered these beautiful women. They were too young to die. They'd had so much of their lives ahead of them. I wasn't much older.

My heart went out to their families, but my job wasn't about getting sentimental. It was about bringing killers to justice.

Jack pointed the cigarette at the three of us, sweeping it back and forth. "Study your copy of the case files, and when we touch down, we'll pick up a couple of rentals at the airport and go straight to the scene. From there, we'll discuss our next steps."

CHAPTER 3

TARA DAY LIVED IN A three-story apartment building near the Columbia Mall. The pattern of its brick facade made it appear as if it were freckled. The redeeming aspect to the property was the lush greenery, and each unit had either a balcony or patio. Tara's apartment was on the second floor.

A couple of crime scene investigators were working over her residence, and I suspected they'd be there for hours yet. Collecting evidence in a murder case wasn't a quick job as it was portrayed on TV. It took time and diligence.

The case file told us Tara's time of death was placed between midnight and three a.m. yesterday. Police found her at nine a.m. after receiving a call from her coworker, just as Nadia had said.

A man I pegged as the lead detective met us at the door. His attention went straight to Jack. My boss just had a way about him. His aura demanded acknowledgment. To those on the outside, there would be no mistaking he was the one in charge.

"Supervisory Special Agent Jack Harper?" the detective asked.

Jack nodded and didn't initiate a handshake. Neither did the detective.

"My name's Detective Russell Powers and—" He looked behind him, searching for someone.

A man in his early thirties hurried over, and I recognized something of myself in him. I had a tendency to run late for things, too, and sometimes it felt as if I was constantly playing catch up.

He smiled at us, his eyes shooting straight to Paige. Maybe we were too much alike. As his gaze settled on her, he bit his bottom lip, as if he thought it made him attractive. His nose was bulbous and too big for his face, and his hair was cropped short and came to a point in the middle of his brow. He extended his hand to Paige.

"This is Sam Barber." Powers made the introduction, but it seemed Barber was getting around fine by himself.

He ended the rounds with me. His shake was firm, and the glint in his eyes told me he was interested in staking claim to Paige. I pressed on a grin, doing my best to make it appear sincere.

"So fill us in. What are we looking at here?" Jack asked. It was part of his tactic. He preferred to be briefed at the scene. He didn't like relying on what came to us secondhand through reports. He liked to hear it from the detective's mouth.

"We've got a female victim. Tara Day. I assume you know most of what we do at this point."

I fought a smirk. Powers wasn't one to play the game, either. He and Jack must have been separated at birth. Like Jack, Powers had a hardened gaze and scowl lines around his mouth. Powers seemed to be in his forties while Jack was in his early fifties. Powers's hair was receding on the sides, leaving a rounded patch of hair in the middle of his head. Jack had a full mop of hair.

"Hmm." Jack brushed past Powers into the apartment. The rest of us followed. It was clear that Jack wasn't impressed with Powers's lack of cooperation.

The layout of the place was simplistic with a galley kitchen to the left of the entry. A living area was straight ahead. The furniture was basic and low-end. Maybe even used.

Powers guided us down a side hallway. "She was found in the bathroom."

The bedroom was on the left, and the bathroom on the right. Powers stopped outside the door. It was compact with the sink and toilet squeezed next to a regular-sized bathtub.

"It's a tight space," I said, verbalizing my observation.

"It is. The killer didn't have much room to work with, but as you know, she wasn't killed here," Powers said.

"She was suffocated in her bed," Zachery pitched in. He knew this from the case file.

"Based on the state of the bed—the sheets were all tangled up—that's the way we're leaning."

"So, afterward, he dragged her lifeless body to the tub?" I asked.

"Your name again?" Powers's eyes were sharp and lasered in on mine.

"Special Agent Fisher."

The hint of a simper twitched Powers's lips. It wasn't hard to surmise what he was thinking—possibly career envy. After all, detectives never had *special* added to their job titles. It wasn't just that, though. In this case, there was derision and judgment painted on his expression. Too bad if the man thought it was egotistical. I had worked hard for the title and had two months before my probation period was over and it was officially mine.

"Well, *Special Agent* Fisher, first he dressed her in a wedding gown, then he placed her in the tub."

"And the dress was hers?" Paige asked.

Barber entered the conversation. "It seems to be. We found the box it would have come in."

"While the gown and ring were hers, the veil wasn't a match to the dress," Powers said.

"Something borrowed?" Paige asked.

"I noticed that in the case file. Its design was different from the dress," Zachery said.

"That's right. The veil had a rosebud wreath, and while her dress had intricate lace rose patterns, there were no buds. It also had a tinge of yellow to it."

I glanced at Paige. "Sounds more like *something old*. It also goes back to what was mentioned about him recreating what he had seen."

Jack shot me a look to keep quiet. There would be plenty of time to discuss the case once we left here.

Powers looked between Jack and me. He caught Jack's glare but didn't bother pressing for more about what I had said. I was thankful to him for leaving it alone.

"Have you found her fiancé?" Paige asked.

"Not yet, but we are looking into that," Barber answered.

"We'll take it from here," Jack said to the detectives. "Has the family been notified?"

"They will be this morning. We weren't able to get in contact with them yesterday," Powers responded. "The medical examiner is expecting you tomorrow for the autopsy. He's quite confident on cause of death, though. The killer got on top of Tara and suffocated her."

"Compressive asphyxia," Zachery added.

Powers appeared about as pleased to be interrupted as Jack did when it happened to him. "That's right. He'll also have all the forensic evidence cataloged for you then."

"Detective?" An investigator came toward our group, her gaze on Powers. She held a plastic bag with a slip of paper inside. "We just found this." She paused, acknowledging the rest of us. Her cheeks flushed, seemingly shy around new people.

"These people are special agents with the FBI." Powers looked at me as he gave the generic introduction. He wanted to make sure I didn't miss the *special* part. "This is Tammy."

"Hi." Tammy rushed to continue. "This receipt was found in her kitchen garbage can. It's dated for last night at seven."

Powers took the bag from her and examined the receipt. He then extended it to Jack, and Jack passed it on to us.

I read the name of the bar, Down the Hatch. The cashier number was 007. Tara's tab came to fifteen dollars. It was a detailed receipt showing two apple martinis. The time stamp, as Tammy had noted, was seven o'clock at night. Early by most standards. Did she meet the unsub at the bar?

I handed the evidence bag back to Tammy, and she left to file it.

Jack addressed me and my colleagues. "Let's see what we can find out at that bar."

Also available from
International Best-selling Author
Carolyn Arnold

BLUE BABY

Book 4 in the Brandon Fisher FBI series

Where light meets darkness...

Happiness is elusive for many, but from the killer's standpoint, it's something he creates. And he's determined to get it right...at least one more time.

The murders were one year apart, but the similarities have the interest of the FBI. Both victims were found in their tubs, dressed in their wedding gowns. But that's not the worst of it. When a third body is found, Brandon Fisher and his team make the chilling discovery that more than the killer's method of operation connects the women.

**Available from popular book retailers or
at carolynarnold.net**

CAROLYN ARNOLD is the international best-selling and award-winning author of the Madison Knight, Brandon Fisher, and McKinley Mystery series. She is the only author with POLICE PROCEDURALS RESPECTED BY LAW ENFORCEMENT.™

Carolyn was born in a small town, but that doesn't keep her from dreaming big. And on par with her large dreams is her overactive imagination that conjures up killers and cases to solve. She currently lives in a city near Toronto with her husband and two beagles, Max and Chelsea. She is also a member of Crime Writers of Canada.

CONNECT ONLINE
carolynarnold.net
facebook.com/authorcarolynarnold
twitter.com/carolyn_arnold

And don't forget to sign up for her newsletter for up-to-date information on release and special offers at carolynarnold.net/newsletters.

13210035R00137

Printed in Great Britain
by Amazon.co.uk, Ltd.,
Marston Gate.